P9-DOF-653

Emma Dilemma and the Soccer Nanny

Dad

McClain

Emma

Annie

Lizzie + Ira

Tim

Mom

Emma Dilemma and the Soccer Nanny

by Patricia Hermes

Marshall Cavendish Children

Other **Emma Dilemma** Books

Emma Dilemma and the New Nanny
Emma Dilemma and the Two Nannies

Text copyright © 2008 by Patricia Hermes
Illustrations copyright © 2008 by Marcy Ramsey

Special thanks to Patiricia Reilly Giff, Joan Elizabeth Goodman,
and Karen L. Swanson

Marshall Cavendish Corporation
99 White Plains Road
Tarrytown, NY 10591
www.marshallcavendish.us/kids

This book is a work of fiction. Names, characters, places, and incidents are
products of the author's imagination and are used fictitiously. Any resemblance
to actual events or locales or persons, living or dead, is entirely coincidental.

Library of Congress Cataloging-in-Publication Data

Hermes, Patricia.
Emma dilemma and the soccer nanny / by Patricia Hermes. — 1st ed.
p. cm.
Summary: When Emma and her brothers and sisters want to get a kitten and
another ferret, and Emma wants their nanny to be the chaperone on her soccer
team trip instead of her mother, the children decide to go on strike to try
to force their parents to meet their demands.
ISBN 978-0-7614-5301-7
[1. Nannies—Fiction. 2. Family life—Fiction. 3. Soccer—Fiction.
4. Pets—Fiction. 5. Strikes and lockouts—Fiction.] I. Title.
PZ7.H4317Ems 2008
[Fic]—dc22
2007034990

The text of this book is set in Souvenir.
Book design by Virginia Pope
Editor: Margery Cuyler

Printed in China
First edition
10 9 8 7 6 5 4 3 2 1

Marshall Cavendish
Children

For Elizabeth and Michael Nastu,
with love
— P.H.

Contents

Chapter One
A Middle-of-the-Night Plan

"Marmaduke!" Emma whispered. "Cut it out."

She was peering over her brother Tim's shoulder at the computer screen and holding Marmaduke, her pet ferret, tightly in her arms. Marmaduke was nibbling on the shoulder of her pajamas. He had pulled loose a little blue ribbon and was sucking on it, trying to slurp it into his mouth and tuck it inside his cheeks. Emma tugged the ribbon free. It was all wet and slimy. Yuck! She quickly set Marma-duke down on the floor.

And then she remembered. The door! Marmaduke would escape in a second. Emma could just picture him running down the stairs in the dark, and Woof, their great big poodle, chasing after him. She ran to the door, but it was okay. The door was shut tight. Then Emma remembered that she had shut it when she had come into Tim's room just a few minutes ago. Good. She smiled. *Very mature*, she told herself. *Mature* was her newest, most important word, a better word even than *grown-up*. It meant that she was super, super grown-up. Mom and Daddy had agreed that she was so mature, they had let her join the traveling soccer team! In just over a week, the team was going on its first trip, to Washington, DC, for a championship game. The girls would stay at a hotel and everything! Emma could hardly wait.

She watched Marmaduke crawl onto the bed. He turned around and around as if he were making a nest, ready to go to sleep. Emma looked over her brother's shoulder again.

"Check once more, Tim!" she said. "See if her plane's landed yet."

"It's not," Tim said.

"How do you know?"

"Because I already tried it a dozen million times. Daddy told me the flight number. He told me the airline. See? Right here?" He put one finger on the computer screen. He read out loud, "Flight 1759 from Shannon Airport is due at five o'clock this morning."

"Right!" Emma said. She pointed to the clock in the corner of the computer screen. "And see! It's five after five."

Tim looked, too. "Okay," he said. "Still, she has to get off the plane and get her luggage and get a cab and all that stuff like Daddy always does."

Daddy was an airline pilot, so Tim and Emma knew all about those things. Still, Emma sighed. She wanted to see Annie so badly. Annie was coming home. Home to them.

Annie was their nanny. She was the best nanny in the whole wide world. She had been their nanny for only a few months, but already Emma loved her more than anything. Annie had been gone for three long weeks, gone to Ireland to visit her sisters. Today she was coming back, and even though it was the middle of the night—well, nearly morning—Emma and Tim just couldn't sleep. Emma needed Annie now more than ever, for a whole lot of reasons.

The main reason was that once Annie came back, she might get to be one of the chaperones on the DC soccer trip, even though Mom had already said no. Mom said Annie could go on later trips, but not on this first trip, since Mom wanted to go herself. She said it was so she could learn more about soccer and the team. Emma thought that, really, her mother just wanted to keep an eye on her. That made Emma so mad. First, Annie knew everything about soccer. She even used to be on the Irish national team. And Mom hardly knew a soccer ball from a shin guard! Second, Annie knew how to handle bad stuff—like Katie. And third, well, there was the business about the team's good-luck charm.

Maybe Annie could persuade Mom to change her mind. At least, Mom listened to Annie a whole lot more than she listened to Emma.

"Tim?" Emma said now. "Let's put up the banner. Annie will love it."

The banner was rolled up by Emma's feet. Tim had made it on his computer. Emma had helped. And the little kids—McClain, Ira, and Lizzie—had all added stuff to it. Tim was ten years old, and Emma, nine, so they were both pretty good at computers. Tim, especially, was a computer pro.

The banner said, "WELCOME HOME, ANNIE. WE MISSED YOU." It also said, "DON'T EVER GO AWAY AGAIN." McClain, who was five years old, had made Emma add that last sentence. McClain had also drawn a picture of Annie and her wild red hair. In the picture, everything about Annie was red— Annie's face and clothes and everything. She looked as if she were on fire.

The twins, Ira and Lizzie, had scribbled some colors and pictures on the banner, too. They weren't quite three years old, but they were super smart. And they never stopped talking. Ira said his scribbles were a picture of Annie's plane. To Emma, they looked more like a giant bug. Lizzie had scrawled a line of colors. She said it was a rainbow.

Tim turned away from the computer. "Now? Mom and Daddy will wake up."

"No, they won't," Emma said.

"They might," Tim said.

"Nah," Emma said. She shook her head. She could tell that he wanted to hang the banner now, too. Emma marched toward the door. "Come on. We'll tiptoe up to Annie's apartment and string it in front of her windows. She'll love it."

"No way!" Tim said. "We'll put it across her door—the *outside* of her door. We're not allowed up in her apartment. You know that."

Emma sighed. But it would be such a cool surprise! She could picture Annie coming home and finding the banner stretched across the windows, or maybe her bed, or something.

Annie had her own apartment on the third floor of their house. Their house was very big and very old. Sometimes Annie let the kids come visit her upstairs. But Mom and Daddy had strict rules: The kids could not go up to Annie's apartment unless they were invited. And they could never go up there if Annie wasn't home. Annie's apartment was Annie's *home*. Hers alone. That's what Mom had said about a zillion times.

Emma swallowed hard. She had broken that rule before. But nobody knew. She just hoped it would be all right now. She really *tried* to do things right. But she had messed up a little lately. Like she had taken Marmaduke to school when she wasn't supposed to, and he had bitten a kid. And then a while back, she had called Annie's sisters in Ireland and told them Annie was getting married, only she wasn't. The reason Emma had done that was to keep Annie from leaving for vacation. Her plan hadn't worked, though. Still, it had turned out all right. And now, Annie was coming home.

Emma looked down at her feet. She had put on her frog slippers. The frogs were staring up at her. They looked very solemn.

"But it would be such a cool surprise!" Emma said.

"It wouldn't be right, though," Tim said.

Tim was her best friend and the best brother in the whole world. But sometimes she got bored with how good he was.

Emma stared down at the frogs again. They stared right back. She wiggled her toes. They seemed to nod at her. She looked at Tim.

"Okay," she said. "Still, Annie wouldn't mind, I bet."

"Mom and Daddy would," Tim said.

"Okay, okay!" Emma said. "We'll just put it up in the front hall." And then she had a better idea. "No, I know! Let's put it up on the outside of the house, maybe on the front door. She'll see it the minute she gets out of the taxi or the car or whatever."

Tim frowned. He looked out the window.

Emma looked out, too. It was getting just a little bit light out. The streetlights were still on, but the sky was a teeny bit brighter. Mostly, though, it was pretty black out there.

"It's dark out. And cold," Tim said.

"So? You've got a bathrobe. And a coat."

"Okay," he said slowly. "You're sure Mom and Daddy won't get mad?"

"Why would they?" Emma said. She looked at her frogs again. "It's not like we're going up into Annie's apartment or anything."

One of the frogs winked at her.

"We'd never do that," she said.

Chapter Two
Welcome Home, Annie!

"Okay," Tim said.

He got up and put on his bathrobe. He tied the sash tightly. Then he went to his closet and got his ski jacket. He put it on over the bathrobe and zipped it up.

While Emma waited, she thought about the soccer trip and how excited she was. She sometimes messed things up, but soccer was one thing she knew she was pretty good at. Her best friend, Luisa, was on the team and she was good, too. But there was one bad thing—Katie. Katie was really, really mean and a ball hog. She also played the same position as Emma. Emma was first string and Katie was only second string. But the bad thing was that Katie was getting better. The coach had even put Katie in Emma's position during the last home game, and Katie had scored. *Three times!*

Still, their team lost the game.

It was partly because Katie wouldn't pass to anyone. But it was mostly because Marmaduke hadn't come with them. When Annie was there, they brought Marmaduke to the games and set his cage on the sidelines. Whenever they brought him, the team won. All the girls patted Marmaduke's nose for good luck before each game. With Annie in Ireland, though, there had been no Marmaduke because Mom had said she wouldn't babysit a ferret on the sidelines. And Daddy had been on one of his trips.

Emma figured that if Annie were allowed to be the chaperone, she would bring Marmaduke to the away game, even though it meant taking him to a hotel. But Mom definitely would never allow that. Mom didn't like it when Marmaduke escaped from his cage, and she'd worry he'd get loose in Washington. And then what? So Emma hadn't even asked. She just knew ahead of time what Mom would say.

Now Emma watched Tim go to his desk to get some tape. He picked up the banner and frowned at Emma. "Aren't you going to get a coat?"

Emma shrugged. "Nah. We won't be out that long."

They both tiptoed into the hall. Emma peeked at the door to Mom and Daddy's room. No light was coming from underneath. Her parents were asleep. She and Tim tiptoed down the hall. They almost tripped over Woof, who was asleep on the rug. He scrambled to his feet and padded after them.

They started down the steps, avoiding the creaky ones. In the front hall, Emma turned the big lock on the front door. Woof bounced around. He seemed excited to be getting a super-early early-morning walk.

"Quiet, Woof," Emma whispered to him.

The door was heavy, and it squeaked a little, but not much. Emma pulled it open.

The cold night air rushed in. Emma wrapped her arms around her middle to keep warm. Maybe she should have put on a coat.

"Watch out!" Tim yelled suddenly.

Emma turned.

It was Marmaduke. He was scurrying past Tim's feet.

Woof barked.

Marmaduke raced for the open door.

Woof raced after him.

"Woof!" Tim yelled.

Marmaduke was already outside on the top step.

Emma reached for Marmaduke. He scurried down to the next step and leaped toward the grass.

Emma practically flew through the air. She landed right on top of him. There! She had kind of squashed him, but he wasn't flat or anything. She scooped him up and held him close.

"You stupid ferret!" she cried, panting. "You awful, stupid ferret." But then she kissed the top of his little head. And next she said, "Stop it, Woof!"

Woof was barking like crazy. Tim was holding Woof's collar tightly, but Woof was prancing up and down, straining to get at Marmaduke. He always did this when Marmaduke got loose. It was a game they played. Marmaduke would get out of his cage, and Woof would chase him around the house. Woof never hurt him. They were good friends. Marmaduke even slept curled up next to Woof when they got tired of playing chase. But they had always played chase inside. Never outside.

Emma was very glad that she had caught Marmaduke before he ran off and got lost in the dark.

Tim looked at Emma. "Maybe you should put Marmaduke back in his cage so Woof will hush. He's going to wake up the whole house."

"Okay," Emma said. "But wait for me. Don't hang the banner till I come back. Maybe we can hang it from the tree by the street."

She turned and started up the steps. She stopped. She turned back. She stepped closer to Tim. "Uh-oh," she said.

"What?" Tim asked.

"Look," Emma said. She nodded at the house. "I think we're in trouble."

Together, they watched.

The whole house was suddenly lighting up. First the upstairs hall. Then the downstairs hall and living room. Next, the front door opened.

There was Daddy. Beside him was Mom. They were both in their pajamas and bathrobes, the ties trailing. Daddy had a big club in his hand—no, not a club, a big heavy flashlight.

Mom and Daddy stared at Emma and Tim.

For one moment, Daddy shut his eyes. He shook his head slowly back and forth, back and forth. "I'm not even going to ask," he said.

"Well, I am!" Mom said. "What in the world are you doing?"

Emma moved even closer to Tim. And then she noticed something. "Tim?" she whispered, poking him with her elbow. "Tim. Look!"

A car was coming down the street, its headlights shining in the dark. It was a big car. It was a big black car. It was the kind of car that took people to and from the airport. It was the kind of car that took Daddy to his job as an airline pilot.

It was the kind of car that would bring Annie home.

"Annie!" Emma cried.

She leaped down the steps and raced to the sidewalk, her froggy slippers flapping.

Tim raced after her. Together, they stood on the curb, Emma hopping up and down, still clutching Marmaduke tightly. Tim was very, very still, as if he were holding his breath. Woof was standing alongside, leaping and barking. And then the car pulled up and stopped in front, and the door opened, and Annie—yes, it was really Annie!

"Annie!" Emma yelled. "Annie! You're home."

Annie stepped out and opened her arms. Emma ran and tumbled into them. Tim did, too.

Mom and Daddy came down the steps, even though they were in their pajamas and robes. Daddy picked up the banner that Tim had dropped, then picked up Annie's bags, and they all hugged and hugged.

"Oh, me dears!" Annie said. She looked so happy, as if she were even crying, she was so happy. "How I've missed all of you."

Emma hugged and hugged Annie, squishing Marmaduke a little between them, but she knew he didn't mind. He loved Annie, too. Emma thought she'd never been happier, not ever.

And then, even though she hadn't meant to say it, the words just popped out of her. "Annie," she blurted out. "Annie, you're going to be a chaperone on the team trip to DC, okay?"

Chapter Three

Annie Has Presents— and a Plan

Mom put a hand on Emma's shoulder. "Emma!" she scolded. "Enough."

She didn't seem really mad, though. Everybody was just so excited to have Annie home. Once inside, they talked and hugged some more, and the little kids, Ira and Lizzie and McClain, came tumbling downstairs. The twins climbed onto Annie's lap, and McClain stuck to her side like glue. Annie gave them each presents from Ireland. Emma's was an awesome soccer shirt from the Irish national soccer team. Emma couldn't wait to show it to Luisa.

Then they all had breakfast, and Daddy asked a million questions about Ireland, and Mom wanted to hear about Annie's sisters, and Ira and Lizzie begged to hear about the "sheeps." Ever since Annie had moved in and showed the twins pictures of the sheep in Ireland, the twins couldn't stop talking about them.

Emma was dying to talk to Annie about Katie and how she was ruining everything and how she wasn't a team player at all! But with the whole family there, Emma couldn't. She did ask about the chaperone thing once, though—well, maybe two times—or three—and Mom got annoyed. So Emma didn't ask again. She just begged and begged to be allowed to stay home from school, for this one day, please, please, please! Mom said no. Tim asked, too, but he asked only once.

When it was finally time to get ready for school, Emma was not happy, not at all. "It's not fair!" she said. She said it as if it were two words—*fay-yer!* She looked at the little kids, all lumped together on Annie's lap. She looked at Marmaduke, cuddled in Annie's lap, too, sound asleep. "How come they all get to stay home with Annie?" Emma asked.

"You know why," Mom said. "Now, go on and get dressed. And if you're smart, you won't do anything to make me remember that you and Tim were out in the middle of the night." Mom was smiling when she said that, but Emma could see she meant it.

Emma knew Mom was right. It was lucky that she wasn't in trouble after being outside while it was still dark with Marmaduke in pajamas. She smiled to herself. The way she had said that inside her head, it sounded as if Marmaduke had been outside in his pajamas.

"I'll be here when you get home!" Annie said, smiling at Emma. "And we'll have a fine time. We can talk and catch up on everything then."

"I don't want to catch up later. I want to catch up now!" Emma said.

Daddy put his arm around Emma. "Go on up and get dressed or maybe I'll remember, too, that you were running around outside in the dark. You'd better not do that on this soccer trip."

Emma looked up at him. "I would never do that. Annie wouldn't let me."

Daddy didn't answer. He just smiled and shook his head.

"Daddy?" Emma said. "You said way long ago that Annie would come to my away games! She knows soccer and . . ."

Daddy held up his hand. "Enough!" he said. "Yes, that's true. Annie can go with you to all the rest of the games. But Mom wants to go to the first one. We've been over all this. Now go and get dressed."

Emma made a face at him, but it wasn't a mean face. She leaned against him for a minute. She really loved Daddy, even when he made her mad.

She loved having him home. She was glad that he wasn't on one of his piloting trips right now. She also knew he was worried that maybe soon he wouldn't be having any piloting trips. He said his airline might go on strike, and that meant nobody could work.

"Maybe you'll want to wear your new soccer shirt to school?" Annie suggested. "I'll bet that old Katie doesn't have anything like it."

"Yes!" Emma said. "I could, couldn't I? Oh, why didn't I think of that!"

She turned and raced into the hall and up the steps to her room. Tim followed behind. He was looking down at his Game Boy, playing with the new game Annie had given him.

Emma hurried to get dressed so she could have a few more minutes with Annie. She picked out her favorite pink pants with the flowers stitched on the pockets and an undershirt because she was still freezing from being outside. Over everything, she pulled on the soccer shirt. She looked at herself in the mirror.

The shirt hung way down past her knees. It almost looked as if she were wearing a dress. Still, it was very cool looking. It was green, with white and red stripes on the sleeves and shoulders. She twisted her head around, so she could look over her shoulder at herself. There was a huge number 1 in white on the back of the shirt. *Very* cool.

And then she remembered something. Today was Friday. Friday was assembly day. The students were all supposed to wear white shirts on Fridays, and they weren't supposed to wear jeans. Emma thought it was a pretty dumb rule. She stepped back and looked at herself again. Well, the shirt was partly white. At least, some of the stripes were white and there were a lot of them. And they were fat stripes, too. Also, the number 1 was white. And she wasn't wearing jeans.

She picked up her backpack and opened her door. In the hall, she met Tim coming out of his room. He was wearing khaki pants and a white shirt with a collar. He frowned at her.

"Won't you get in trouble?" he asked.

She shook her head. "Nah," she said.

Tim looked worried. He often looked worried.

Emma ignored him and raced down the stairs and into the back playroom where everybody had gone after breakfast, jabbering with Annie.

Daddy was shaking his head at the news on TV—airline strike news. Mom was sitting at the big work table, sorting through soccer forms for the trip. Mom had her office down the hall in the back of the house, where she did her work planning exhibits for the museum. But for family stuff, she usually worked here in the playroom. Now she looked up when Emma came in.

"Emma," Mom said. "Did you know that there are two girls on your team who are allergic to bee stings?"

"Really?" Emma said. She thought that was funny, especially since their team was named the Hornets.

"Yes. Really. I have all these medical forms," Mom said, picking up a blue slip of paper. "The girls need to supply their EpiPens, and we chaperones need to learn how to give them shots in case they get stung, even if they have parents there, too."

"Gross," Emma said. "You mean real shots, like doctors do?"

Mom nodded. "Yes, real shots. And then there's a tour planned of some of the Washington monuments—at least, if there's no second game. And we need permission slips and player badges with the girls' pictures." Mom sighed. "Maybe I should have thought twice about volunteering to manage this game. But when the team manager broke her ankle . . ." Mom sighed again.

Emma just smiled. She looked up at Annie.

Annie smiled back. She stood up, gently sliding

the little kids off her lap and putting down the sleeping Marmaduke carefully on the sofa. She took Emma by the shoulders and looked at her. "Now, doesn't that wee shirt look handsome on you!" she said. She turned Emma around. "I believe you've grown in the three weeks I've been gone!"

Emma smiled at Annie. She hadn't grown, not that fast. But she liked that Annie had said that.

Annie pulled Emma close and walked with her out into the hall. "I just thought of something," she said quietly. "Today's Friday, isn't it?"

Emma nodded.

"Your shirt?" Annie said.

"It's okay," Emma said.

"You sure?" Annie said.

Emma nodded again. "Sure. Look. There's lots of white on it."

Annie looked worried. "You don't want to get into trouble," she said. "Not just before the big trip."

Emma sighed. "I know. And Annie, I need you on that trip so much. Katie is being so mean. She's trying to get my spot on the team."

"Oh my. We can't have that happen, can we? But now, away with you. Go change your shirt like a good lass."

Emma felt her shoulders droop. She so much

wanted to show off her shirt. Annie was right, though. She didn't need to get into trouble now. "Okay," she said. "But I'll take it with me. I can put it in my backpack. I can show *everybody.*"

"Brilliant!" Annie said. "Then after school, we'll talk about that Katie. And we'll work on your soccer skills." She smiled. "And while you're at school, I'll work on your mother."

She looked through the door at Mom in the playroom.

Emma looked, too.

Mom looked frazzled. More than frazzled. She was actually holding her head and pushing her hair up with both hands, like people do when they're upset. Emma had never seen anyone actually do that, except on TV.

"Your mother maybe doesn't know that I studied nursing in Ireland," Annie said.

"You did?" Emma asked, wide-eyed. "Really?"

"I did," Annie said. "Now scoot. Not to worry. I have a plan."

Emma hoped so much it was a good plan. If Annie really were trained as a nurse, that would count for a lot with Mom. Especially with the way Mom was looking just now.

Emma smiled. She turned to go upstairs and change. Suddenly, though, she had a thought.

About needles and shots. She stopped. She went back and looked through the door to the playroom.

"Mom?" she called. "Is Katie one of the allergic ones?"

Mom shuffled through the papers. She shook her head. "No," she said. "Vanessa Samson and Courtney Bland."

"Oh," Emma said.

Too bad, she thought.

Chapter Four
New Crazy Pets

Emma just knew the school day would never end. She wanted so much to get home to find out if Mom had agreed to let Annie be the chaperone. And she needed to talk to Annie about—everything!

Still, the day wasn't as slow as Emma had expected, because a few good things happened. When she showed her new soccer shirt to her best friend, Luisa, Luisa said she would die for a shirt like that. She thought it was totally, totally cool. Emma showed the shirt to other kids, too. Lots of them were on soccer teams, and almost every kid loved it. All but Katie. She just shrugged.

"Jealous," Luisa whispered to Emma. "Katie's jealous."

And then, the second best thing was this: At the assembly, Emma learned that Mrs. Adams, her teacher, had been given a big award. She had been named Teacher of the Year. That meant she was the best teacher in the whole United States!

That made Emma smile. She loved Mrs. Adams. In fact, she thought Mrs. Adams wasn't only the best teacher in the United States. She was the best teacher in the whole entire world!

But then show-off Katie did something really show-offy and gross. When they got back to class, Katie pranced up to the front of the room, very important looking. She stood close beside Mrs. Adams. She turned and faced the class. "Let's all clap for Mrs. Adams!" she said. "Teacher of the Year!"

The whole class started applauding. Jason whistled, and some of the boys stamped. Mrs. Adams looked shy, but Emma could see she was pleased. Emma applauded, too. But she also glared. Not at Mrs. Adams. But at Katie.

Katie was disgusting.

Finally, though, the day was over, and all the kids trooped onto the buses to head home. Tim and Emma rode the bus together, and when they got off, they raced up the walkway. They couldn't wait to see Annie!

Before they got to the house, though, they saw Annie and all the little kids in the van parked in the driveway. Annie rolled down the window.

"Hop in!" she said. "We've been so excited waiting for you."

Emma and Tim jumped in back.

"Where are we going?" Emma asked.

"To get Kelley!" McClain yelled.

"Our cat!" Ira said. "We're getting our new cat."

"*My* cat!" McClain said.

"But it's going to live in *my* house," Annie said. "Right?"

Emma smiled. How could she have forgotten? They had found a stray kitten before Annie had left for Ireland. McClain had fallen in love with it and had named it on the spot: Kelley. Mom and Daddy said they couldn't have a cat. But they didn't say *Annie* couldn't have a cat. So their vet, Dr. Pete, had kept Kelley until Annie got back from Ireland. The cat was going to live upstairs in the apartment, at least for a while. Mom was always saying how Annie's apartment was her very own home—so that should be fine, right? Except Emma wondered if Mom had thought about cats when she'd said that.

"Does Mom know yet?" Emma asked. "Is she home?"

"No," Annie said. "She's in the city at a museum appointment."

"Did you ask her?" Emma asked. "About the soccer trip?"

Annie turned around and smiled at Emma. "I think I made a bit of headway," she said.

"What's that mean?" Emma asked.

"It means she was very taken with my nurse's training."

"So she said yes?"

"Not exactly," Annie said. "But almost. I helped her a wee bit with the forms."

"Let's go, let's go!" McClain said, bouncing up and down in her seat. "I want to get Kelley."

"All right, we're ready!" Annie said, turning to the front. "Everybody's seat belt on?"

"Mine's on," Emma said. She settled down in her seat. Yes! Annie had said *almost*. That meant yes; Emma was sure. She was so excited.

When they got to Dr. Pete's, Emma helped Ira and Lizzie unbuckle their seat belts. Then they all tumbled out of the car. Once inside, the kids huddled around the cage where Kelley was sleeping. Dr. Pete reached down and lifted Kelley out. "Whose cat is this?" he asked, smiling.

McClain held out her arms.

Dr. Pete handed Kelley to her. Then he looked down at his clipboard and started talking about Kelley and what food and stuff she would need.

While he talked, the little kids hovered over the fat, gray kitten, petting her and touching her fur. Tim stood near McClain, patting her hair every so often, the way the little kids were patting Kelley. Emma thought Tim was just about the sweetest brother in the whole entire world.

Emma knew she wouldn't get a chance even to touch Kelley right then, so she walked into the other room where Dr. Pete kept his animals for adoption. Dr. Pete was sort of an animal-rescue person. He collected all sorts of injured animals and made them better. Then he tried to find people to adopt them.

There were rabbits and dogs in the cages. Through the window, Emma could see the outside pen and, in it, there was even a deer. Emma walked all the way to the end of the aisle. There were so many beautiful animals—a small, funny yellow dog, another cat, two black rabbits. Emma was amazed. She hadn't even known that rabbits came in black. All the animals looked sad, as if they wanted to be taken home. Emma wished she could take every single one of them. She stopped and spoke to each one. She stuck her finger through the wire of their cages and petted their fur.

And then, at the very end of the aisle, Emma saw

him—Marmaduke! Marmaduke, her ferret! What was he doing here?

She sank down on the floor beside the cage. "Marmaduke!" she cried. "Marmaduke! What happened? How did you get here? How . . ."

But then she realized it wasn't Marmaduke. It wasn't. This ferret wasn't quite as dark gray as Marmaduke. But almost. And his head was a teeny bit smaller. But it could have been his twin. It looked exactly like him.

The cage wasn't locked, just latched tightly. Emma lifted the latch. She leaned in and scooped out the ferret. She held him tightly in her arms. "You're a Marmaduke twin!" she whispered to him. "You look just like Marmaduke. Oh, Marmaduke would love you! I wish he could see you."

Then, just like Marmaduke, this ferret leaned his head up close to her. He nestled himself under her chin, rubbing up and down, as if he wanted to make friends. He nibbled on her sweatshirt. He sucked the tie into his mouth.

Gently, she pulled it out. "Don't do that," she said softly. She patted his rough head. He leaned into her shoulder. Oh, if only she could take him home. He could keep Marmaduke company.

Marmaduke was lonely. That's why he kept escaping from his cage. And this ferret looked lonely, too.

"Do you want to come home with me?" Emma whispered. "Do you? I have another ferret, Marmaduke, and you could be friends."

He snuffled, just like Marmaduke did, as if he were saying, "Yes, I would love to be Marmaduke's friend."

Emma got to her feet, the ferret still locked in her arms. Oh, if only she could have him. But what would Mom say? Mom was always getting mad at Marmaduke for escaping. Would she really say okay to another ferret? Well, probably not. But if they kept each other company, they wouldn't need to escape. She could tell Mom that. Slowly, Emma walked back down the aisle to the other room. She could hear Dr. Pete and Annie and McClain and the others. Through the door, she could see McClain still hugging Kelley.

Everybody looked up when Emma came to the door.

"Oh, I see you found my sad little friend," Dr. Pete said. "I've been looking for a good home for her. You wouldn't want to take her home, now, would you?"

"Yes," Emma said. It was almost a whisper. "Yes, I would." She looked at Annie. "Could I? Please?"

Annie looked at Dr. Pete. She looked at Emma. She looked at the ferret in Emma's arms. "Oh my," she whispered.

Chapter Five
A Big Fat Mess

Emma was bursting with the news. She had tried calling Luisa, but all she got was an answering machine. She didn't want to talk to a machine, so she sat down at her computer to write an e-mail.

To: Luisalovessoccer
From: Emmalovesferretstoo
I have a new ferret. From Dr. Pete. Mom doen't know yet. So this is how it werked out. Annie sed she'd keep my new ferret for a while. Till Mom says I can have her. And Annie's keeping Kelley too our new cat. I hav to go. Mom's calling dinner. Annei's eating with us. She mite even go to Washington DC with us I hope. I think almost for sure. She helped Mom a lot today. Rite back.
P.S. I named her Marshmallow.

Emma reread her message. It looked funny. She knew some of the words weren't spelled right. Spelling wasn't the thing she did best. She thought of running spell-check but decided not to. Luisa would understand.

She ran downstairs, thinking about Marshmallow and how happy she was. But she also felt a little worried in her stomach. She kept telling herself it was all right. It really wasn't *her* ferret—at least, not yet. Annie had agreed that Emma could take Marshmallow home. But only if Marshmallow lived upstairs in Annie's apartment for a while. Emma thought that was a good plan. Mom and Daddy couldn't really get mad if Marshmallow stayed at Annie's, could they?

But now there was a new problem. Who would care for Kelley and Marshmallow if Annie went to DC? Tim, maybe? Marshmallow would be all right in her cage. All she'd need would be food and water, and the trip was only for two days. But Kelley would be running free around Annie's apartment, and she was just a kitten.

It was a whole lot to worry about, but Emma decided to push away all her worry thoughts. It was Annie's first night home, and everything was going to be just fine. Usually, Annie didn't eat dinner with the family. Most nights, she was happy to go upstairs to her own apartment and relax at the end of the day. Emma knew Annie loved them, but she also knew Annie needed a break sometimes, too— at least, that's what Mom had explained. Today, though, since it was Annie's first day back, Mom had invited Annie to dinner and Annie had said yes. At dinner they could talk about the soccer trip.

Now as Emma ran downstairs, she heard a huge ruckus going on in the dining room. Mom was trying to persuade Lizzie and Ira to get up into their high chairs. They were both standing on the floor, as if they were cemented to it. They were staring at Annie. Ira's face was all dark, like a thunderstorm about to burst. Lizzie was holding onto the edge of the table. Her knuckles were white from holding on so hard, but her face was very red.

"Oh, me dears!" Annie said. "Now what is the big fuss all about?"

"That!" Lizzie said, pointing at her high chair.

"Hate that!" Ira said.

Annie went around the table to the twins. She looked at Mom. "May I?" she asked.

Mom nodded.

Annie bent and picked up Ira with one arm and Lizzie with the other. "Now, what's this all about?" she asked. "What's so bad about a high chair? You can see so much more from up there."

"No!" Lizzie said.

"No *babies!*" Ira said.

"Honestly," Mom said, "they change by the minute. Now they think they're too big for high chairs." She smiled at Annie. "We've missed you, Annie."

"I've missed you, too," Annie said. "All of you."

Annie hugged the twins and whispered something in their ears. They looked at her, then at their high chairs.

Annie whispered again.

"O-tay!" Ira said. He scrambled out of Annie's arms and down into his chair.

Lizzie scrambled down into her chair, too.

Emma wondered what Annie had said to them. Probably promised something—maybe that they could go up and visit Kelley and Marshmallow after supper. Annie had said she'd tell Mom and Daddy about the pets at supper, but that the little kids shouldn't say anything until then. Annie would know just the right way to say it, but the twins could really mess up if they blurted it out too soon. Emma just prayed that they would remember to keep quiet.

After everyone was seated, they all bent their heads and said a prayer. Afterward, everybody started talking at once. Daddy talked about how his airline might be going on strike, and Tim wanted to hear all about it. Tim always worried about

Daddy's flying. Daddy explained that it just meant that people lined up outside the airline office holding signs. Sometimes the signs said that the airline was acting unfairly to the pilots and not paying them enough. Other times, the strikers were demanding different stuff, like more time off. It was called a picket line, and you weren't supposed to cross that line. So maybe Daddy couldn't go to work till the people went away.

"Do the strikers get what they want?" Emma asked.

Daddy laughed. "Sometimes," he said. "Not every-thing, usually. They negotiate—get a little, give a little."

Then Mom wanted to hear more about Annie's sisters and what Ireland was like. The little kids were bashing each other with spoons, pretending they were dueling. And McClain was grinning to herself, probably thinking about Kelley.

And Emma—well, she just wanted Mom to say that Annie could be the DC chaperone. Definitely. Finally, Emma interrupted all the babble.

"Mom?" she said. "Mom? Did you know that Annie was a nurse once? Well, sort of a nurse?"

"Yes, we talked about that today," Mom said, smiling.

"And she's never been to Washington, DC,

before," Emma said. She didn't even know if that was true. The words just sort of popped out of her.

"Is that true, Annie?" Mom said.

Annie nodded.

"Hmm," Mom said. She looked across the table at Daddy. "Maybe that would be a nice benefit for Annie," she said.

Daddy nodded. "Yes. It sure would."

"So you guys have decided?" Emma said. She was practically jumping around in her seat. "Really? Annie can go?"

"Well," Mom said. "We did say a while back that Annie *might* be your chaperone."

"I *told you!*" Emma said.

Mom nodded. "I know. But I still want to go the first time myself." She paused and seemed to be thinking about something. And then she said, "But in some ways it makes more sense for Annie to go. Since she knows soccer and has a bit of a medical background."

"Hooray!" Emma said.

"Hold on!" Daddy said. "We haven't decided for sure. I know Mom *really* wants to go. Anyway, Annie, would you be comfortable with a whole lot of kids?"

"Da-ad!" Emma interrupted. "*We* have a whole lot of kids! And it's not like she'd be in charge of the kids all by herself. Each girl brings a parent. The only difference is, she'd be the team manager for just this one game. And that's only 'cause Mom volunteered."

Mom shook her head. "And why I did that, I don't know," she said. "I guess I thought I'd be . . . I don't know what I thought."

"That's okay," Emma said. "Annie can do it. Can't you, Annie?"

But before Annie could reply, there was a huge ruckus, even bigger than the one Ira and Lizzie had been making. This one was coming from upstairs. Above their heads. It was the sound of little feet— scampering, scooting, madly tearing-around little feet. Lots of them. And kind of a yowling sound, too, muffled, as if it were far away. But definitely a yowl. Like a cat.

Emma sucked in her breath. She quickly looked at Mom. She looked at Tim. They both looked at Annie.

The feet kept going 'round and 'round. Had Marshmallow gotten out of her cage? Was she going to hurt Kelley? Or would Kelley hurt her? And . . . uh-oh! . . .

Everyone had stopped talking and was listening.

"Emma! Is that Marmaduke?" Mom asked, turning to Emma.

"No!" Emma said. "He's in his cage. Honest."

"It doesn't even sound like that noise is coming from Emma's room," Daddy said, his head tilted to one side. "It sounds like it's coming from the attic."

"Oh goodness!" Mom said. She looked wide-eyed across the table at Daddy. "Squirrels, I bet. They've probably gotten into the attic! At least, I hope it's the attic, not Annie's apartment. Remember that time when . . ."

Emma remembered. There was the time that Annie had almost fallen off a ladder trying to climb into the house when a squirrel had . . .

Suddenly, there was a much bigger sound, a thump, a bump, then a squalling, yowling.

"A cat?" Mom said. "Could we have a *cat* in the attic? How . . ."

Annie stood up. "It's all right," she said softly. And then, before she could make another single move, a cat came racing into the room. It was a fluffy cat. It was a fat gray kitten.

It was Kelley!

Behind Kelley came a ferret, a skinny silver ferret.

Marshmallow!

Chapter Six
The Secret Gets Out

For one weird moment, nobody moved, nobody spoke, not Annie or Mom or Daddy or the kids or anybody. Everyone was totally silent and still.

They just stared as Marshmallow circled the table, chasing Kelley. Suddenly, Kelley stopped. Marshmallow stopped. Kelley turned. She hissed. Her fur stood on end. She crept toward Marshmallow, one little paw at a time, up in the air, then down. Marshmallow backed up.

Woof came galloping into the dining room, barking crazily. Mom reached down and grabbed him by his collar. She stopped him, but she didn't stop his barking. Kelley kept stalking Marshmallow. Marshmallow kept backing up.

Woof kept barking madly.

"Hush!" Mom said to him.

"Just stay calm, everybody!" Daddy said. Slowly,

he stood up from the table. "Nobody move. It's only a stray cat that got in somehow. Emma, you catch Marmaduke. I'll catch the cat. Everybody else, stay put."

"Careful!" Mom said. "He could be rabid!"

"No, no, it's all right," Annie said softly. "It's just a wee kitten. She's not rabid at all. She's as sweet as she can be."

But Daddy didn't seem to hear. He moved around the table carefully, bent as if he were a cat himself that was going to pounce.

He didn't get a chance to pounce, though, because Annie got to Kelley first. She just took a few steps, crouched down, and scooped Kelley up and into her arms. "There you go, wee one!" she said.

At the same time, Emma scrambled after Marshmallow. She caught her easily. Marshmallow hadn't even tried to run away. She'd just stood frozen on the floor, trembling, looking terrified. Emma got to her feet, pressing Marshmallow against her chest. She could feel Marshmallow's little heart thudding like crazy because she was so scared. Emma wondered if ferrets had heart attacks. She hoped not. "It's all right," she whispered to Marshmallow. "This happens a lot. You'll get used to it." She patted the ferret gently.

"Okay, now!" Daddy said, after both Marshmallow and Kelley had been scooped up. "Somebody tell me what's going on here. Is that your cat, Annie?"

"Yes," Annie said. She then looked at McClain. "Sort of."

"Sort of?" Daddy said.

"It's all of our cat!" Ira said. He was standing up in his high chair, trying to get his seat belt off.

"Mine, too!" Lizzie said.

"It is not!" McClain said. "It's just mine."

"I don't understand," Mom said. "Annie said . . . what *did* you say, Annie?"

"Well," Annie said slowly. "It's just—well, after we found her, we decided . . ."

"You *found* her!" Mom said.

"Yes," Annie said. "Remember? Dr. Pete kept her for me. She's had all her shots."

"Dr. Pete?" Mom said. She let go of Woof's collar and Woof went dashing off to sniff around Annie and Kelley. "Annie," Mom went on. "Annie, you just got home today. Did you bring the cat with you from Ireland? Did you take him straight to Dr. Pete?"

"Oh no!" Annie said. "I wouldn't bring me a cat from Ireland. That wouldn't be at all right, now, would it? There would be a long quarantine. Me sister did that with her rabbit once. Poor little creatures have to stay in cages at the airport or somewhere for so long. Indeed, it's not fair to them at all."

"But then . . . ?" Mom said.

"It's Kelley, Mom!" McClain piped up. "We found Kelley! Remember, Mom? Before Annie went away, remember how we found a cat, and we told you about her? Remember? Her name's Kelley. She's mine."

"Oh no!" Mom said. "Absolutely not! I told you that you could not have a cat! We have one dog and one ferret, and that's plenty. More than enough! I'm sorry, McClain, but you cannot have a cat. Not that cat or any other cat."

McClain's little face got all crumpled up.

"Mom!" Emma said. "It's okay. McClain doesn't really *have* a cat. Annie has a cat. Annie's keeping the cat."

"Right! For *me!*" McClain said. "And she's keeping . . ."

McClain looked at Emma. Then she looked at Marshmallow.

Emma looked down at Marshmallow, too. Her heart was thumping as hard as Marshmallow's. She took a deep breath. Marshmallow was right out here in plain sight. Everybody thought she was Marmaduke. They had to keep thinking that. "It's okay, Marmaduke," Emma muttered, just loud enough, she hoped, for Mom to hear.

She snuck a look at Tim. He looked worried.

Annie sat down, lowering Kelley into her lap. She put one hand on Woof's head and patted him while he sniffed hello at Kelley. "Let me tell you the whole story," she said. "See, what happened is we found Kelley, like McClain just said. You remember that? And while I was gone, Dr. Pete kept him."

"He's not a *him!*" McClain said. "He's a *girl!*"

"Hush, McClain," Mom said. She turned back to Annie. "So you decided to keep him—her? The cat?" Mom asked.

"Yes," Annie said. "I hope it's all right?"

Mom didn't answer.

"You did say it's my home," Annie went on. "And you didn't say no pets—I mean, no pets for me. She'll stay up in my apartment. She won't come down at all. I promise."

Mom looked over at Daddy. She shook her head. Emma knew what she was thinking.

Daddy frowned and shook his head, too.

Emma looked from Daddy to Mom. She hoped Annie wasn't in trouble. She also wondered how Marshmallow had gotten out. That cage must not have been strong enough. Or maybe Annie had left her door open?

44

"Down!" Lizzie demanded suddenly. She was standing up in her high chair and looking at Annie. "I want to pet Marshmallow."

"Me, too!" Ira said. "You promised."

"Marshmallow?" Mom said. "I thought the cat was Kelley."

"It is. That's Marshmallow!" Lizzie said, pointing at the ferret in Emma's arms. "Annie said I could pet her after supper."

"Wait a minute!" Mom said. "What did you say?"

Lizzie looked away. She chewed on her lip. "Nothing," she muttered.

Emma bent her head. She hugged Marshmallow close. Marshmallow was still trembling. Emma felt a little shaky, too. She couldn't look up. She was so mad. Little kids could never keep a secret!

"Emma?" Dad said. "Annie? Somebody tell me what's going on here."

Emma took a deep breath. She still didn't look up.

"Emma!" Mom said. "Look at me. Is that Marmaduke you have there?"

Emma looked up. She swallowed hard. "Uh, no," she said. "Not exactly."

"Not *exactly*?" Daddy said. "What does that mean?"

"It means . . . Marmaduke's upstairs," Emma said.

"I see," Daddy said. "And what ferret do you

have in your arms there? Or am I just imagining that you're holding a ferret?"

"No," Emma said. "You're not imagining it. It's a real ferret."

Daddy shook his head. He looked almost as frazzled as Mom had looked this morning over the soccer forms. "Then if that's not Marmaduke, who is it? What is it?" he asked.

"It's Marshmallow," Emma said. She turned Marshmallow around, so Mom and Daddy could see her little face. "See?" she said. "It's not Marmaduke. See how she's a whole lot skinnier than Marmaduke? See how her head is littler? It's even kind of pointy. This isn't Marmaduke. This is Marshmallow. And, Mom and Daddy, honest, she'll keep Marmaduke company so they won't escape, neither one of them. You know how lonely Marmaduke gets, and that's why he gets out of his cage all the time. But two of them . . . "

"Emma!" Mom burst out. "You can't possibly think you can keep *two* ferrets! When one is always on the loose?"

"No, no!" Annie interrupted. "Emma won't have two ferrets. This is my ferret. For now. I mean, I'm keeping her upstairs in my apartment. With Kelley." She looked at Mom and Daddy as if she were trying to smile, but Emma thought she looked a little worried. "I thought maybe a wee cat could use a wee ferret as a playmate?"

"Wonderful!" Mom said. "Just wonderful!" Mom pushed her hands through her hair, just as she had done that morning. "Like we need more wild creatures in this house!"

"Oh, but they're not wild," Annie said. "They're very sweet. And children learn so much from pets. They really do, even wild ones. Now, me sisters and me, we found a stray fox and once even a skunk . . . "

Daddy held up his hand. "Annie," he said. "I think you'd be wise not to say more. Now, listen. Take these creatures out of here. Upstairs to your place. And keep them there until we decide what to do."

"Daddy!" Emma said. "Wait! Wait. We can negotiate."

Annie smiled. But Daddy didn't.

"Some things are not open to negotiation!" he said—meanly, Emma thought.

He looked across the table at Mom, shaking his head. "Can you believe it?" he said. "And she's just been home one day?"

"I know," Mom said. "What next?"

Chapter Seven
Up in Annie's Apartment

Emma lay in bed for a long time, staring at the ceiling. She thought about the list of bad things that could happen:

1. Mom and Daddy could make Annie take Marshmallow and Kelley back to Dr. Pete's pet shelter.
2. Mom and Daddy could say that if Annie wanted to keep pets, she couldn't live up in the apartment anymore. And then Annie would have to live somewhere else, and that wouldn't be the same as having her in the house with them.
3. Or, if Annie didn't want to live somewhere else, then she'd have to give back Marshmallow and Kelley, and that would

break McClain's heart. It would break
Emma's heart, too.

Emma wasn't afraid that Mom and Daddy would
fire Annie and get a new nanny—at least, she
wasn't too afraid. Mom and Daddy had made it
clear before Annie left for Ireland that Annie was
family. "You don't get rid of family," Daddy had
said. Still, Annie had just gotten home from Ireland
that very day, and look at the big fat mess they
were in already.

And now, what about the soccer trip? Emma
needed Annie with her. Mom was nice, of course.
But she wasn't any fun. Annie was fun. But more
than just fun, Annie could help with the Katie
problem and all the soccer problems and, of
course, with Marmaduke, the good-luck charm.

Emma turned over. She lay flat on her back and
tried counting sheep, as Annie had taught her to
do. But it hardly ever worked. The sheep were
supposed to move nicely toward a fence and jump
over it. But hers always got twisted up or they
tumbled over or something. They were just a mess.
This time, they played a game, leaping over one
another's backs, then falling down in a heap.
Emma tried lining them up again. They lined up
backward. It was just not restful.

Finally, Emma got up and brought Marmaduke into bed with her. She made sure that her door was closed tightly so that Marmaduke couldn't escape in the night. They snuggled together. Emma told Marmaduke all about Marshmallow and how she'd introduce them soon. She told him that Marshmallow was kind of timid, so not to scare her too much till they got used to each other. And she told him about the mess she'd gotten into that day. Marmaduke fell asleep in the middle of it. But Emma was still wide awake.

The moon was shining through her window, slipping shadows across her books, her toys, everything. She looked up at the shelf that held her dolls and saw the bride doll. She remembered the time she had pretended to Annie's sisters that Annie was getting married. Emma realized she hadn't even had a minute to talk to Annie about her sisters or anything. She hadn't told her about the latest soccer game and how they had lost because of Katie and because of Marmaduke's not being there. And she hadn't told her how she now felt guilty that she had persuaded Annie to bring home Marshmallow. She felt terrible because now Mom and Daddy thought Annie was irresponsible. How could Emma fix all this?

Emma couldn't stand it any longer. Quietly, she

slipped out of bed. She picked up Marmaduke and put him back into his cage and snapped the lock shut. He didn't even wake up. Then she went out into the hall. She looked around. It was dark and still. No light was coming from under anyone's door. The whole house was sound asleep. Even Woof was asleep on the hall rug and didn't look up at her.

Softly, slowly, Emma tiptoed down the hall. At the very end of the hallway, toward the back of the house, was a door, and behind the door, the stairway that led up to Annie's apartment. It was closed tightly. But there was a bit of light coming from under the door. Annie was awake.

Emma's heart was pounding hard. She knew she wasn't supposed to do this. Mom and Daddy had made strict rules about Annie's privacy. Still, she needed Annie. She really, really did. Very quietly, carefully, she opened the door.

She listened. No sound. No TV. No music.

"Annie?" Emma whispered. She listened harder.

Nothing. Yes, something. Annie was talking softly. Was she on the phone?

"Annie?" Emma called, a bit louder.

"Emma?" Annie called back softly. "Is that you?"

"Yes. Can I come up?"

"Of course you can, me dear!" Annie said.

51

Emma scrambled up the stairs.

Annie was sitting on her sofa. Kelley was asleep on the pillow beside her. Marshmallow was curled up in Annie's arms, also asleep. Annie must have been crooning her to sleep. That's what she called it when she sang to the little ones when they had trouble falling asleep.

Annie carefully set Marshmallow down. She held out her arms to Emma. "Come here," she said softly.

Emma ran to Annie. She plopped down beside her, being careful not to sit on Marshmallow or Kelley. And then, as if she were as little as Ira or Lizzie or even McClain, she practically fell into Annie's lap. She told Annie everything—how much she had missed her and how lonely it had been without her, and how she worried about Marshmallow and how McClain really, really wanted Kelley. And she told about how she worried that Annie might have to move away. She told about how she had broken a rule— how she had tiptoed up to Annie's apartment when Annie was gone, just to sit on her sofa for a minute and pretend Annie was there, and how she hadn't meant to break into her privacy or anything. And then she told again about soccer and about Katie. How unfair it was that Katie got to be left wing, striker, the one who scored, and Emma was stuck with being goalie. Emma was the high scorer on the team, and now Katie was just taking over, and Emma so much needed Annie's help and . . .

And Emma realized that for some weird reason she was crying a little bit. She didn't really feel that sad. At least, she hadn't thought she was that sad. Maybe it was just relief. Maybe it was just . . . she didn't know what. But Annie's arms felt awfully good.

"Oh, Emma!" Annie said, when Emma had finally wound down and couldn't think of one more thing to say. She wrapped her arms around Emma even more tightly. "It's all right! We'll work all this out."

"But now Mom and Daddy think *you're* irresponsible," Emma said, "because of Marshmallow!"

Annie laughed. "And don't forget Kelley!" she added.

Emma sniffled and sat up straighter. Then, for a moment, she couldn't help giggling. She reached around and picked up Marshmallow. Marshmallow was still sound asleep, but she snuggled into Emma's neck.

"Mom sounded plenty mad," Emma said. "And Annie? This week we'll play our last home game. Monday."

"I can't wait!" Annie said. "And I'll bring along

Marmaduke, our good-luck charm."

"We're going to really need him in DC," Emma said.

"I know!" Annie said. "You'll have to bring him along. Your mother can check the hotel's policy about pets. But I'm sure it's no problem since he's in a cage."

After a minute, Emma looked up at Annie. "Know what?" she said. "If we win this last game, then we move to the higher level in DC. And if we win there, we get a trophy. I've never gotten a trophy."

"Never?" Annie said.

Emma shook her head. "Never," she said. "I've never been best at anything."

"Is that right?" Annie said. "Well, we're just going to have to make sure you get one this time, won't we?"

Emma nodded. "Annie?" she said, feeling shy. "Annie, do you think I can ever be best?"

"Best?" Annie said. "You mean best at soccer?"

Emma looked down. She snuggled Marshmallow closer. She nodded. She did mean at soccer. But she meant more than that. It seemed as if everybody in the house was best at something—everybody but her. The twins were best because they were so little and so smart, and people were always staring at them and saying how smart they were. McClain was the cutest with her curls and her funny, mad ways. And Tim was just plain good—really, really good and responsible, besides being a genius at computers. And Emma? She sighed. She wasn't really best at anything.

She didn't think she could say these things, though, not even to Annie. So she just said, "Do you think Mom and Daddy will let you go? To DC?"

"Maybe," Annie said. "But, Emma, I do understand your mom wanting to be with you since this is the first trip."

"Why?" Emma said. "She just wants to come along to make sure I don't mess up! And you know what else? She doesn't listen to me. Neither does Daddy."

Annie held Emma closer. "Oh, that's not true. They listen."

"But they still do just what they want," Emma said. "And nothing changes."

Annie laughed softly. "Well, we'll work together to change some things," she said. "It's going to be all right, I think."

Emma sucked in a deep breath. She leaned against Annie, squeezing Marshmallow between them. She felt relieved, maybe even a tiny bit happy. She wasn't quite sure why. She knew that everything was maybe not going to be all right. And she worried about Annie saying, "I think." But she did feel a little better. Maybe just because Annie was home. Maybe because, right now, that's all that mattered.

Chapter Eight
A Rotten, Horrible, Terrible Day

The next day and the next day after that were absolutely rotten and awful and horrible and stinky. Annie was off on Saturdays and Sundays, but most weekends, she came down to visit the kids, at least for a little bit. And she almost always had Sunday supper with them. Not this weekend, though. She stayed up in her apartment the whole entire time. Mom said she was probably exhausted from her trip and the change in time zones, and so she was sleeping. Also, Mom said, a reporter was coming from the local paper to interview Annie about Ireland, so she wouldn't even be having Sunday supper with them.

Daddy was grumpy about his airline and the strike and kept turning on the news on TV or else checking it out on his computer. His face was dark and worried. Mom was snappish and crabby and wouldn't even talk about the soccer trip and chaperones—the one time Emma dared to ask.

The twins were mad that they couldn't visit Marshmallow, and they each had tantrums, but not at the same time. One would finish and the other would start. They did it five different times.

McClain acted like a little bear because she couldn't see Kelley. She ran to her room and slammed things around and then locked herself in, even though Mom had threatened her with terrible things if she did that—like taking away her favorite dolls for a whole week. McClain didn't even seem to care. She slammed stuff around more than ever. On Saturday afternoon, she had a complete meltdown in the hall and cried till she began to hiccup. Late in the afternoon, Emma found her asleep in a heap in front of Annie's apartment door.

Even Tim was out of sorts. He stayed shut up in his room, working on his computer and listening to music on his iPod. He was nice when Emma knocked and went in, but she could see that he really wished she'd go away. She knew he was worried about Daddy and the strike. He said he had looked up strikes on the Internet, and sometimes airline strikes went on for weeks. He said that he was afraid that if that happened, Daddy wouldn't get paid.

On Sunday morning it was raining, and Daddy suggested that they go to a movie, but no one could agree on which one to see. So Daddy went to the video store and rented a different movie for each kid—five of them! They had to take turns watching them in the playroom, and even then, they all fought over whose DVD they should watch first. Tim went to his room and looked at his on his computer.

By Sunday afternoon, Emma was feeling terrible. She missed Tim. She missed Annie. She even missed the little kids, since they were glued to the DVD. She hated it when everyone was mad and upset.

After lunch, she went up to her room and closed the door. She got out her favorite book, *The Secret Garden*, and curled up on her window seat to reread it. She thought it was the best book anyone had ever written. It was all about this girl who had no family, and she met this boy who was a big fat pain, and they became very, very good friends, and the boy stopped being a big pain anymore. Along the way, they met an old gardener, and he became their friend, too, and then they met a boy named Colin, and they found a secret garden where they could hang out together. And everything worked out well.

Emma didn't start the book at the beginning this time, though. The beginning was kind of slow, and even a little bit sad, so she skipped to the part where the girl, Mary, found the sick boy. But she had read only a little bit when she put the book down.

She wasn't even having fun reading it this time! How come in books, things worked out for people? But in real life, they didn't? She stared out the window at the rain. In real life, moms got mad and little brothers and sisters had meltdowns, and best-friend brothers sulked, and daddies worried about being on strike, and . . .

And she jumped up from the window seat. She suddenly had an absolutely brilliant idea.

She ran out of her room and down the hall to Tim's room. She knocked and opened the door. "Tim?" she said. "Can I come in?"

But she was already in.

He turned around. He paused the movie on his computer.

"What?" he said.

"I have a plan!" Emma said. She sat down on his bed. "Listen." And she outlined her plan.

By the time she was finished, Tim was frowning. Tim always worried before he finally went along with one of her ideas. Well, sometimes he went along. This time, he went along faster than she had expected. "We could try," he said. "Want me to get the little kids?"

Emma nodded. "Yeah. We'll meet in my room."

"You'd better be the one to get McClain, though," Tim said.

Emma nodded. She knew why he'd said that. Even though McClain had the worst temper in the whole world, Emma was the one person in the family who could usually calm her down.

Tim ran downstairs to the playroom to get the little kids, and Emma ran to McClain's room. The door was closed, but she could hear McClain banging on something—only she wasn't slam-banging the way she had the day before. There was just a little tap-tapping. Emma knocked. Then she tried the handle. It was locked.

"Go away!" McClain said. And then she said, "Who is it?"

"It's me, Emma," said Emma. "And you know you're not supposed to lock your door."

"You can't come in," McClain said. She started banging again.

Emma stood on tiptoe and got the key from the place where Mom kept it—on the ledge above the door. Daddy said that hiding the key there was the solution to the door-locking problem; otherwise, Mom and Daddy would have to get a whole new door that didn't have a lock.

Emma unlocked the door and went in.

McClain was sitting in the middle of her room, her dolls spread out around her on the rug. Very methodically, she was bopping each one on the head with the mallet from her toy drum. She wasn't smashing them to bits or anything. She was just giving each one a severe bop on the head.

She looked up at Emma. She didn't even seem surprised. She knew all about the key—she just couldn't reach it herself, although once Emma had caught her standing on a chair outside the door, trying to get it. But she couldn't. She was too little.

"Come on, Clainie," Emma said, using her pet name for her sister. She went over and sat on the floor beside her. "We're having a kids' meeting in my room."

"A meeting? Why?" McClain asked.

"To fix things. To make things better."

McClain looked up. She shook her head, and all her curls jounced around. She looked really, really sad. "What things?" she said. "Mom won't let me have Kelley."

"She might," Emma said. "Now, come on, Clainie. I have a plan."

"For what?" McClain said.

"I'll tell you all about it when we get to my room," Emma said. "Everybody's been acting terrible. I know how to make things better."

"You can't," McClain said sadly. "Kids can't make stuff better. Not even you."

"Wanna bet?" Emma said. "Kids have rights, too."

"Nope!" McClain said.

"Yup," Emma said.

She took McClain's hand and tugged her to her feet. "Come on. Let's go."

McClain let Emma take her hand. "Do you mean I might get Kelley? Is that what?"

Emma grinned. "Yup. That and other stuff."

"Really?" McClain said. "You mean it?"

"I mean it," Emma said.

"How?" McClain asked.

"Simple," Emma said. She grinned at her sister. "We kids are going on strike."

Chapter Nine
The O'Fallon Kids
Go On Strike

When they had all gathered in Emma's room, Emma outlined her plan. Actually, she didn't have a plan. But she started planning as she talked. And Tim helped. He had lots of ideas, mostly because of having looked up strikes on the Internet.

First thing, she and Tim explained to the little kids what a strike was. Tim did most of the explaining, because he was good at that kind of thing and had done the research. Mostly, what he said was that the kids would make signs. Then they would march around the house holding the signs. The signs would say what it was they each wanted. And they should practice saying something, too, all together—such as: parents are unfair to kids—or something like that.

"Right!" Emma said. "But we're not going to march around the house. We're going to march on the street *outside* the house!"

"On the street?" Tim said. "But then everybody will see us!"

"Duh!" Emma said. "That's what we want. Right? Isn't that what a picket line is for? Daddy said picket-line people make demands. If we're outside and everybody else sees us, and we're all saying, 'Unfair!,' then Mom and Daddy will *have* to do something."

Tim made a face. "They might get mad, though."

"They're already mad," McClain said.

"Doesn't matter," Emma said. "We definitely have to go outside."

"Well, maybe," Tim said. "I guess. Anyway, we'll make the signs. And if we don't get what we want, then we will—"

"Go on strike," McClain said.

"We're already on strike," Emma said.

Tim made a worried face at Emma. "What will we do," he asked, "if they don't meet our demands?"

Emma chewed on the inside of her lip. "Maybe not do our chores?" she suggested.

"You'll get in trouble for that," McClain said.

"I know!" Ira said. "We'll scream!"

"Loud!" Lizzie said, clapping her hands.

"Like that does any good!" Emma said. "No, it has to be something important. To make them notice. Something like . . ."

"No kisses!" Lizzie said.

Emma laughed. She patted Lizzie's leg.

"Not come downstairs for dinner?" Tim said.

Emma turned and grinned at him. She was surprised. Tim was usually so into being good and obeying. She wondered if just thinking about being on strike had made him brave all of a sudden.

"Maybe!" she said. "We could just stay in our rooms and refuse to come out."

"Not me," Ira said. "I'd get hungry."

"Anyway," Emma said, "remember that strikers negotiate sometimes. If Mom and Daddy say no, we can say we'll negotiate. Let's just make the signs first. Later we can decide what we'll do if we *don't* get what we want. So, what are our demands?"

"Kelley!" McClain said right away. "I want Kelley."

"I want Marshmallow," Ira said.

"Me, too," Lizzie said.

"Okay," Emma said. "You can put that on your signs. But you know that Marshmallow is *my* ferret."

"We know that," Ira said.

"He knows," Lizzie said.

"Okay," Emma said. "And my sign says I want

Annie to go to DC with me." She turned to Tim. "What do you want?"

Tim sighed. He bit his lip. "For Daddy's airline not to go on strike," he said softly.

Emma sighed. "Yeah," she said. "But we can't make that happen. Or not happen. So you have to choose something else."

Tim nodded. He thought for a minute. "Okay," he said. "I want a cell phone."

"Not fair!" Emma said. "I want one, too."

"Well, I said it first," Tim said. "And we can't both ask."

Emma made a face. But Tim was right. It wouldn't be fair for them both to ask. "Okay," she said. "I guess." But she didn't like it. Not one bit.

"I'll share it with you," Tim said. "If I get it."

Emma smiled at him. "Okay," she said. "Now, let's make up the signs. McClain, you go to the playroom and get those huge pads of paper and markers. And get string and tape. We're going to need string to hang the signs around our necks."

"I'll get stickers!" Lizzie said. "I have puppy stickers."

"I have rockets," Ira said.

The little kids scooted away. They were back in just minutes with the supplies. Then everyone sat in a circle on the floor of Emma's room.

Right away, McClain stretched out flat, face down. She grabbed a fat blue marker and started coloring huge blue circles on a piece of paper.

Lizzie began pasting stickers all over her paper. Then she started pasting them on her arm.

Ira started by tracing his hand on the paper. But he got bored before he had hardly even started. "Emma?" he said. "Can I get Marmaduke out of his cage?"

Emma sighed. But then she said, "Okay. Why not?" She got up and made sure the door to her room was shut tightly. Then she went and unlatched the cage.

Ira bent down and lifted Marmaduke out very, very gently. Emma watched him. She was always surprised how nice little kids could be, and then how mean. Ira was gentle with Marmaduke all the time, but he was sometimes really, really mean to Woof. He'd pull Woof's itty-bitty tail, and sometimes he even pulled at Woof's legs when Woof was stretched out sleeping. And though Lizzie never hurt the pets, sometimes she got mad at Ira and bit him.

Now Lizzie jumped up and joined Ira on the floor by the cage. Marmaduke climbed up onto Lizzie's lap, and Lizzie squealed.

"Okay, gang," Emma said. "Pet him just for a minute. Then you have to get to work."

"I'm already at work," McClain said. Her page was now almost all dark blue, except for a little red dot up in one corner and a black dot up in the other.

"What are you making?" Emma asked.

"The sky," McClain said. "And see this here? This is my robin. And this one is Daddy's plane. He didn't go on strike yet, so he's still flying up there."

"Oh," Emma said. She wasn't sure that the sky and a robin had anything to do with their being on strike, but maybe the plane did. Anyway, it didn't matter much. Later Emma and Tim could write in McClain's demands about Kelley.

After a while, Ira and Lizzie abandoned Marmaduke and put him back into his cage, and everybody finally finished their signs. Tim helped all three little kids letter the words for their "demands." The next step was to tape the string to the back of the paper.

It took practically the whole afternoon to finish the signs but finally, they were done. Emma stood up and looked out the window. The rain had almost stopped, but it was still gray and drizzly. "Okay, everybody," she said. "Go get your coats.

And Ira, put your shoes on. We're going outside."

"I have to ask Mom!" Lizzie said, darting toward the door.

"Stop!" Emma said. "No way. It's a surprise. We're going to line up outside the house. We're a picket line, remember? Mom and Daddy will look out and be so surprised."

"But I'm not supposed to go out without asking," Lizzie said.

"You're asking me," Emma said. "And I say okay."

"Really?" Lizzie said.

"Really," Emma answered. "Now stay right here."

"What if they don't look out?" McClain asked.

Emma glanced at Tim. She hadn't thought of that.

"We'll ring the doorbell," Tim said.

Emma nodded. "Right! We won't wait for Mom and Daddy to look out. We'll ring the doorbell right away, then run back to our places on the sidewalk. And this is what we're going to say: 'Parents are unfair to kids.' Got it?"

They all nodded.

"Parents are unfair to kids," Emma repeated. "Now, all ready? Let's go."

She grinned and started out of the room ahead of everyone else. She held her sign close against her chest. On the very top, above her demands about Annie and the soccer trip, she had printed in big black letters:

The O'Fallon Kids Are On Strike

Chapter Ten

The Green-Bean Lady Comes to Call

It's like herding cats, Emma thought. First, Ira insisted that he didn't need shoes, and when Emma said he *had* to wear them, he got mad. He finally got some, but they were old summer ones without toes and it was fall now. After they'd been outside for two minutes, his little toes turned bright red. McClain couldn't find her coat, so she put on three sweaters and was so bulked up she could hardly walk. Emma thought that if she fell over, she'd never be able to get up. Lizzie had on both shoes and a coat, but then she fell down and scraped her knee on the back step and began to howl. And all this time, Emma and Tim were trying to keep them quiet so Mom and Daddy wouldn't come looking and ask what was going on.

Finally, they were outside and in the backyard. Emma lined them up, one after the other by size, starting with Ira. For some reason, even though they were twins, Lizzie was way bigger than Ira. So he was first, then came Lizzie, and then McClain. Emma should have been next because Tim was a little taller than she was. But Tim said that since this was Emma's idea, she should go to the head of the line in front of Ira.

Emma thought that maybe Tim was a little scared about the whole thing, and that's why he wanted to hang back. But she didn't mind being the leader. Besides, that way, with Tim at the end of the line, he could make sure that the little ones didn't break away and disappear.

At last everyone was ready. They left the backyard and scooted around the corner of the house.

"We all set, gang?" Emma asked, as they stepped out onto the sidewalk. "We know what we're going to do and say?"

"Ready!" Ira said.

"Ready!" Lizzie said.

"I'm not," McClain said.

"What's the matter?" asked Emma.

"My sign hurts." McClain tugged at the string around her neck.

"What'd you do to it?" Emma asked. She looked at McClain. The string of her sign was so twisted up, she was practically choking.

73

"I wanted it shorter," McClain said. "So I made a knot."

Emma rolled her eyes. It took another long minute for Emma to get out the knot. "And don't twist it up again!" Emma said. She took a deep breath. She looked at the little ones. She huffed out her breath. "Are we *really* ready now?"

They all nodded.

"Okay," she said. "So we are going to walk in a line, slowly. We're going to line up in front of the house. And, all together, what are we going to say?"

"Parents are unfair to kids!" They all said it together, but they said it way too loudly.

"Not so loud!" Emma said. "We don't want them to hear, not yet. Mom and Daddy are going to look out and see us, and *then* we're going to say it. Let's hear it once more. But whisper."

"Parents are unfair to kids," they all whispered.

"Perfect," Emma said.

She smiled at them. They all looked so serious.

"Okay, I'm going to ring the doorbell now," Emma said.

"Be careful!" said McClain.

Emma frowned at her. "Why?"

McClain shrugged. "I don't know."

Emma shook her head. "Silly," she said. She

started toward the steps. But just as she did, she saw a car turning the corner and stopping at the curb in front of their house. A tall, skinny woman in a green raincoat got out. She looked a lot like a string bean.

"Excuse me?" she called to Emma. "Is this fourteen hundred?"

Emma nodded.

"The O'Fallons?"

Again, Emma nodded. "Why?"

"Because," she said, "I'm a reporter for the paper *The Citizen*. I'm looking for someone. Does Annie O'Reilly live here?"

"She's our nanny!" Lizzie said. "She just got home. She went to Ireland and saw sheeps."

The string-bean lady smiled at them. Emma thought she didn't look so much like a string bean when she smiled. More like something from the cartoon *Veggies*.

"Yes," she said. "That's why I wanted to interview her. We're doing a piece on Ireland for the travel section." She smiled at the kids then and said, "You kids look like you're on strike or something."

"We are!" McClain said. She pointed to her sign. "I want my cat!"

"And our ferret!" Lizzie said.

"Well, isn't that something?" the lady said. She had a huge bag on her shoulder, and she reached in and pulled out a camera.

"Are you a stranger?" Ira asked.

The lady laughed. "Well, I guess I am. Sort of. To you, anyway. But I'll tell you what. I'll just go inside and talk to your mom and dad first, and then I'll ask for permission to talk to you guys. I'd love to write a story about kids who go on strike. Would that be all right?"

Emma smiled. "Why not?" she said. If it made the papers, Mom and Daddy would *have* to give in, or else people would think they were awfully mean.

She looked at Tim. He looked worried.

Oh, bother, she thought.

She turned back to the lady. "It's all right," she said, waving her hand. "You can ring the doorbell now."

"I hope you don't mind if I just snap a few pictures first," the woman said. And without waiting for an answer, she did just that.

Then she turned, went up the steps, and rang the doorbell.

Emma looked down at the little kids. "Okay," she said. "Now Mom or Daddy will come to the door. Stand right here next to me, okay? Don't move. Right by me. Ready?"

"Ready!" Ira said.

"Me, too," Lizzie said.

They lined up on the sidewalk in front of the house. Ira began bouncing up and down, his little red toes sticking out of his shoes. He was giggling and holding his sign to his chest with both hands.

Next Lizzie started bouncing, too.

her was so bundled up in her sweaters, her face was flaming red, and her curls were sticking to her head. But she held her head very, very high, looking straight ahead, chin out, as if she were in a marching band.

Tim was next to McClain. He stood up just like her. If Emma didn't know him so well, she would think he was calm, but she could tell he wasn't, not at all. His eyes were darting back and forth as if he were in a cage.

And then the front door opened.

"Okay, kids!" Emma said softly. "There's Mom. Now!"

"Parents are unfair to kids!" they yelled. "Parents are unfair to kids."

Mom stepped back, as if she had just stepped on a snake. Then she stepped forward again. She leaned out of the doorway, staring. She shook her head a few times, as if she couldn't believe what she was seeing.

"Let's say it again, kids!" Emma said.

"Parents are unfair to kids!" they all yelled.

Even from the sidewalk, Emma could see that Mom was blinking hard. But it seemed that maybe she was smiling, too. Emma didn't know if that was good or not so good. She did want Mom to take them seriously. But she didn't want Mom to be mad.

Mom turned her head and frowned at the green-bean lady with the camera. Then she swiveled around, and she must have called Daddy, because suddenly he popped up behind her. They stood together, Daddy's arm around Mom's shoulder, both of them looking down the steps at the sidewalk, just shaking their heads again and again.

Ira and Lizzie began waving like mad. Even McClain started to grin and wave.

The green-bean lady snapped away with her camera.

Tim stepped close to Emma. "Emma," he whispered. "What if those pictures end up in the paper? We're toast!"

Emma shook her head. "No, we're not. Don't chicken out. We're not backing down."

"We have to. I mean, what if Mom and Daddy don't agree? What will we do?"

Emma turned and pointed a finger at Tim. "Negotiate!" she said.

Chapter Eleven

More Trouble

It took a long time for the kids to straighten things out and to convince Mom and Daddy that they hadn't called a reporter to take pictures and to tell their story in the newspaper. But finally, everything was explained, and the green-bean lady was invited in, and they all sat down together in the playroom. Annie came downstairs to be interviewed about Ireland, which is why the lady had come to visit in the first place.

Emma learned that the string-bean lady had a name. Her name was Mrs. Beene. Really, honestly, truly. A squiggly little laugh burst out of Emma when she heard that. She quickly put a hand over her mouth and pretended to be coughing. Mrs. Beene asked all sorts of questions—but not of Annie. She wanted to talk to the kids and to hear about the "strike." As Mom and Daddy looked more and more nervous, Mrs. Beene asked about the kids' demands, and about the cat and the ferret, and why the two pets were living up in Annie's apartment.

And then she asked, "Whose idea was this strike, anyway?"

All the kids looked at Emma. There was no way out of it. Emma had to say "mine," and so she did. And then she looked away, because suddenly, she wondered if she had messed up again. Maybe the strike hadn't been such a good idea after all.

She sent a look to Tim.

She sent a look to Annie.

"Well, it was kind of *all* our idea," Tim said.

"But it was Emma's most," said McClain.

"Only sort of," Tim said.

Mrs. Beene took out her little notebook and began making scratchy marks in it. Emma went over and sat on the floor by Annie's feet. She leaned against Annie's legs. Annie put her hand on Emma's hair.

"So," Mrs. Beene said, looking at Emma. "You're a good soccer player? You must be if you are on a traveling team."

Emma nodded. "I am good," she said. And then, because that sounded kind of stuck-up, she added, "Pretty good, anyway."

"Do you have any more home games?" Mrs. Beene asked.

Emma nodded. "Tomorrow. Monday. Four o'clock."

"Well, maybe I'll come and watch you," Mrs. Beene said. "Maybe I could write a story about the best soccer players in the area."

"Really?" Emma asked. She sat up straight. "You would, really?"

"I might," Mrs. Beene said. "We're always looking for stories about the best in every field."

"Oh," Emma said. She didn't know what else to say. She would love to have Mrs. Beene write about her. But then her shoulders slumped, and she leaned back against Annie again. If Mrs. Beene came to a game to write about Emma, she'd probably end up writing about Katie instead. Everybody did. Katie wasn't just a ball hog. She was an attention hog. And where did that leave Emma?

"So, tell me about your demands," Mrs. Beene said. "What's this about soccer travel and chaperones?"

Emma started to answer, but then she stopped. She looked away. Suddenly, she didn't like this Mrs. Beene very much. It really wasn't any of her business. It was family business. And besides, Mom and Daddy were fidgeting and looked as if they wanted to get rid of Mrs. Beene. Emma also knew that Mom and Daddy would have plenty to say to the kids about the strike. Emma wondered if the strike had changed their minds about anything. Like cats and ferrets and soccer.

Daddy stood up and began pacing back and forth. Then he went to look out the window, his back to the room, his hands stuffed in his pockets.

Mrs. Beene didn't seem to take the hint. She turned to Mom. "So, now, Mrs. O'Fallon," she said, "will all the children's demands be met, do you think?"

She said it with a smile, but Emma could tell that she really was curious. And as Emma watched Mrs. Beene's little pencil hovering above the notebook, she could see Mrs. Beene was ready to write down whatever Mom answered.

Mom must have thought so, too, because she didn't say anything for a while. She looked over at Daddy. He didn't look back.

Before either of them uttered a word, Emma spoke up. She had to stop them from saying, *No, never. We're the parents; we make the rules around here,* because that's the kind of thing she knew they might say.

"Negotiations!" Emma said. "During any strike, that's what people do. Negotiate."

"What's that?" McClain said.

"It means, each side gives up a little," Tim said.

"I'm not giving up Kelley," McClain said.

Annie reached out and pulled McClain onto her lap.

"I'm not!" McClain said, and she stuck her lip way out.

"Well, there are many ways to negotiate, aren't there?" Mrs. Beene said. "I mean, maybe Kelley could be half yours and half Annie's."

"You can't cut a cat in half," McClain said.

"They're yucky inside," Ira said.

Mrs. Beene laughed.

"They are!" Ira said. "Right, Lizzie?"

Lizzie nodded. "Inside their mouth. You should see. It's red."

Emma thought that maybe they should change the subject.

Annie must have thought the same thing. Very gently, she slid McClain off her lap. She stood up. "Mrs. Beene," she said. "Why don't we go up to my place? I'll be glad to show you the pictures I took of Ireland."

Mrs. Beene finally got the hint, and she stood up, too. Both she and Annie turned to go. Before they left the room, though, Annie reached down and helped Emma to her feet. She gave Emma a big sweet smile. And a big thumbs-up sign. Then she hugged her close. "You go, girl!" she whispered.

And she left, leaving Emma to face the mess she had gotten them all into. And leaving her with a little courage, besides.

Emma sure needed it. Because as soon as Annie and Mrs. Beene were gone, Daddy turned back from the window. "All right, gang," he said, pointing to the playroom table. "Come on. Over here. Sit."

"Why?" Ira asked.

"How come?" Lizzie said.

"Because Daddy said so," McClain answered. She had her bottom lip stuck out about as far as it could go.

Daddy laughed but Emma didn't. What McClain had said was just so true. And it was the whole problem with being a kid in this house.

Ira and Lizzie looked super grumpy, too, but they scrambled up into two chairs. Mom came over and sat down next to Ira. She was chewing on her lip the way she did when she was worried or upset. Woof bounded over to the table, looking from one to the other. Emma thought even he seemed worried.

"So," Daddy said, looking directly at Emma. "I guess you kids have some things you need to talk about."

Emma nodded.

"Yes?" Daddy said.

Emma took a deep breath. What should she say? How much should she say? She stole a look at Tim, but he wasn't looking back. "It's just that— um, sometimes, um, you don't listen."

"I think we listen plenty," Mom said.

Daddy put his hand on Mom's arm. "Well, let's listen now," he said quietly.

Mom sucked in a big breath. "Okay," she said. "Okay." She shook her head. "And let's hope to heaven that reporter doesn't write something terrible about us all."

"Oh, she won't, Mom!" Emma said. And then, before she could add another single word, Ira suddenly yelled.

"Lizzie hit me!"

"You were pulling Woof's ears!" Lizzie yelled back, glaring at him.

"Was not!" Ira said. He picked up a crayon from the table. He threw it at Lizzie. It hit her right in the head.

Lizzie grabbed Ira's hand. And bit it.

Mom and Daddy jumped up. Mom gathered up Ira. Daddy scooped Lizzie into his arms.

Both kids were howling as if they'd been run over by a truck. Ira was sobbing, and tears were streaming down Lizzie's face.

"Could we finish this talk later?" Daddy asked,

turning to Emma and raising his voice to be heard over the howling.

"How about tomorrow?" Mom said, holding Ira close. He was sobbing so hard he sounded as if he'd break. "Let's talk tomorrow. The twins are exhausted."

Daddy nodded. "Okay?" he asked, looking at Emma.

She nodded. Tomorrow would be fine. The kids *were* exhausted. She was exhausted, too. And kind of nervous and worried.

And now she was sure that the strike had been a bad idea all along.

Chapter Twelve
Emma Loses Out

The next day was Monday, the day of the soccer game. Daddy had been called in to fly to Ireland on a quick overnight trip, since the strike hadn't started yet. That meant he couldn't come to the game. Mom couldn't come, either. She had to stay home because Ira had an ear infection. Mom said she had been really looking forward to the game, too, but Ira's temperature was too high.

That afternoon, Emma and Annie walked to the soccer field together. Emma and the other players had to go early to show their player badges to the ref and to get the lineup from their coach. Emma carried her cleats and the bag with the balls. Marmaduke was in his cage, and Annie pulled him in a little wagon that belonged to Ira.

"Annie?" Emma asked, looking up at her.

"Annie, do you think Mom and Daddy were mad yesterday? About our strike?"

"Oh, I don't think so," Annie said. "But you do need to sit down and have that talk."

"We have to wait till Daddy gets home tomorrow," Emma said. "And, Annie, will you sit down and talk with us?"

Annie smiled. "Of course. If you want me."

Emma nodded. "I want you. Do you think Mrs. Beene will really come today and write about me?"

"I should hope so," Annie said. "She sounded like it." Annie pointed to where the girls were clustered around the coach, Mr. George. "Who are we playing?"

"The Rockets," Emma said. "The Hornets against the Rockets. Remember them? They wear those cool blue jerseys? And they have that Roberta person who's so fast and so big."

Annie laughed. "I remember her," she said. "But you're fast, too. Just watch that you don't run out ahead of the defenders and get offsides. That's the big thing for you to work on. Also, plan your shots carefully. Now, go out there and win! I'll be cheering you on. And if you need me, I'm right here. So's Marmaduke."

Emma sat on the bench and put on her cleats, then ran to where the Hornets were standing. She said hi and smiled at her teammates—Bethany and Courtney and Raquelita and Molly and Vanessa and Margaret Ann and all the others, especially her best friend, Luisa.

She didn't even look at Katie.

"All right, girls," Mr. George said. "This is going to be a tough game, but we can win it. I want to see teamwork. *Pass the ball.* I want to see those assists. Don't think you can do it all yourself."

Emma thought he looked at Katie when he said that. But then she realized he was really looking at her.

She started to say, *I pass!* but decided just to let it go.

Katie was smiling at her. A mean smile.

"Now," Mr. George said, "you all have your player badges?"

They nodded. Each girl had to have a badge with her name and birth date and picture on it. Most of the girls kept their badges on chains attached to their soccer bags so the badges wouldn't get lost. If you forgot your badge or lost it, you couldn't play.

"Okay," Mr. George said. "Get your badges, line up, and show them to the ref."

The girls ran to the sidelines. Emma ran alongside Luisa. On the way, they passed Margaret Ann. She was bent over her bag, frantically searching through it, pulling stuff out. She looked up. There were tears in her eyes.

Emma shook her head. Margaret Ann was a total crybaby. If the ref yelled at her, she cried. If they lost, she cried. She had even cried once when they'd won. And she was forever losing things and forgetting things. Then she cried about that. The weird thing, though, was that she was goalie. That meant she sometimes had to throw herself down in front of the ball as the players charged toward her, and she always got scratched up. But she never cried about that.

Now Emma saw that Luisa had stopped running. So she stopped, too.

"What's wrong?" Luisa asked kindly.

Margaret Ann looked up. She looked frantic. "My badge!" she said. "My player badge. It's gone!"

"What do you mean, 'gone'?" Luisa asked.

"It's gone. Just gone."

"Well, what did you do with it?" Emma asked.

"I didn't *do* anything with it!" Margaret Ann cried. "I had it before, and I set it down here on top of my bag when I put my goalie shirt on, and now it's gone."

"That can't be," Emma said. And then, because she felt bad for thinking mean things about Margaret Ann, she said, "Here, I'll help."

She bent over the bag and began pulling stuff

out. Luisa helped, too. They both emptied it, handing things one at a time to Margaret Ann. Emma even held the bag upside down and shook it. No badge.

"Girls!" Mr. George called. "What's holding you up?"

"My badge. It's gone!" Margaret Ann called.

Mr. George jogged over to them. "How can it be gone?" he said. "You know you can't play if you don't have it."

"I *have* to play!" Margaret Ann cried. "My grandma came all the way from Florida just to see me play today!"

"Well, look!" Mr. George said. "Look in that bag."

"We did," Emma said. "We looked everywhere." She stood up and turned to Margaret Ann. "Are you sure you didn't leave it at home?"

Margaret Ann shook her head. "I know I had it here. When I put on the goalie shirt."

"Maybe you *thought* you had it here," Emma said. "Maybe when you put on your other shirt at home, that's when you had it."

Margaret Ann shook her head. "I don't think so," she said. "I'm sure I had it here." But she didn't sound as sure as she had before.

"I know!" Emma said. "Follow me! Come on."

91

She ran to the sidelines where Annie was standing beside Marmaduke's cage. "Annie!" she shouted. "Did you bring your cell phone?"

"That I did," Annie said. She dug it out of her pocket.

"Thanks," Emma said. She took it from Annie and handed it to Margaret Ann. "Here! Call your mom. Tell her to look everywhere. It's probably in your room."

Margaret Ann took the phone. She looked up at Emma, her eyes flooding with tears. "Thanks," she whispered. "Oh, thanks."

Emma nodded and ran over to Luisa. They followed the rest of the girls and Mr. George to the ref. Katie was the last to line up. She had been talking to her private soccer coach on the sidelines.

"Margaret Ann's mother just *has* to find it," Emma said to Luisa as they waited in line. "What will we do without her?"

"Lose, probably," Luisa said. "How could she have lost her badge? We need her! You know how important a goalie is!"

"We don't need her," Katie said. "Not so much."

"What do you mean, 'not so much'?" Emma said, turning to her. "She's our goalie!"

Katie shrugged. "Well, we have other goalies,"

she said. "You did good as goalie last game."

"No way!" Emma said. "I'm left wing, and you know it."

"And you know I scored three times last game!" Katie said.

"And we still lost!" Emma said.

"Girls, girls!" Mr. George said, holding up his hand. "This is a team! Or, at least, it's supposed to be." He looked at his watch. "Margaret Ann had better hustle."

By then, most of the girls in line had finished having their badges checked. Next it was Emma's turn, then Luisa's, then Katie's. And, finally, Margaret Ann's.

"My mother will be here with my badge in five minutes!" Margaret Ann said breathlessly, looking up at the ref, her face dirty where she had rubbed away the tears. "Honest. Just five minutes. She's looking. I must have left it on my dresser or something."

The ref tapped his watch. "I'll give you exactly five. No more. Then it's game time."

"But maybe I could go in at halftime?" Margaret Ann said.

The ref shook his head. "Against the rules," he said. "You should know that by now."

Mr. George put a hand on Margaret Ann's

shoulder. "Come on, Margaret Ann," he said softly. "Stop worrying. Let's go. Your mom will find it."

"Oh, I hope!" Margaret Ann said.

Mr. George turned and spoke quietly to the ref for a moment, then went to the sidelines and picked up his clipboard. The girls followed him. They stood around silently, looking glumly out toward the parking lot for Margaret Ann's mom. They needed a good goalie. In spite of all her tears, Margaret Ann was good. Super good!

Emma knew they were all worried. But nobody was as worried as she was. She had her fingers crossed behind her back. She knew what would happen if Margaret Ann's mom didn't find the badge. And she didn't even want to think about it.

But Mr. George was thinking—thinking what she wished he wasn't thinking.

"Okay, Emma," he said after a minute, looking up from his clipboard. "If her mom doesn't get here in time, you'll go in as goalie. You did great last week. Katie, you play left wing; Luisa, you be right. We'll manage. Don't worry."

Don't worry? Emma thought. *What do you mean, don't worry? With Katie taking over?*

Across the field, the other team had gathered and were running around, all zippy looking and happy.

"Hurry, Mom!" Margaret Ann whispered. "Hurry!"

Hurry, Margaret Ann's mom, hurry! Emma said to herself.

"No offense, Margaret Ann," Katie spoke up. "But I think Emma's a little better at goal, anyway."

Emma just stared at Katie. She couldn't believe that Katie had said such a mean thing! And then, before Emma could even think of an answer, she heard someone calling from the sidelines.

"Margaret Ann, Margaret Ann!"

Margaret Ann turned. "She's here, she's here!" she shouted. "My mom!"

They all turned and looked. She was there. Margaret Ann's mom. She stood on the sidelines. Both hands spread out. Upturned.

Empty!

Chapter Thirteen
Awful Katie Moves In

By halftime, the Hornets had not scored. But the Rockets hadn't scored, either. It was zero to zero. Emma was in as goalie, and she had made seven terrific saves at goal. Seven! And three of the saves were falling-flat-out-on-her-face kind of saves. She was exhausted, sweaty, and thirsty. She felt as if she had been playing for hours, instead of just twenty minutes.

Emma had played goalie only a few times before. She hadn't realized how hard it really was. She also hadn't realized how good she was in that position. She always seemed to know, before the opposing team even kicked, where the ball was headed and in which corner of the net it would land. And so far, she had been able to get there ahead of it. She had learned that watching a player's eyes helped her know a lot about where the player was going to aim.

Besides feeling exhausted, she had a mean little happy feeling, too. She couldn't help feeling happy that Katie hadn't scored. But she sure wished that somebody would. And she so much wished it could be her.

She dragged herself over to the sidelines and collapsed between Luisa and Margaret Ann.

Margaret Ann looked forlorn. Emma wanted to say, I'm sorry. But she thought that would make Margaret Ann feel worse. It was especially bad for Margaret Ann, since her dad had arrived—too late—with her badge. He'd found it on the floor of his van. So Emma said, "That's a hard position to play."

"I know," Margaret Ann said. "But you're good."

"Thanks," Emma said. And then she added, "But not as good as you."

Mr. George handed out water bottles and orange slices to the girls. They had flopped on the ground everywhere, trying to catch their breaths. Two of the girls lay flat on the grass like rugs. Vanessa and Courtney were flapping their shirts up and down like a pair of huge blackbirds, trying to cool off. Emma leaned against a bunch of soccer bags, using them like pillows. And Katie stood doing stretches, one foot lifted up behind her, grasping it with her hand, stretching out the muscles. She was standing right in front of the bench, looking around, and smiling as if she were being videotaped or something.

Why did she need to stretch? They had been playing for hours, practically.

Emma took a water bottle, sipped, then turned it upside down, pouring it over her head. The water ran through her hair and down her neck and felt awfully, awfully good.

"You okay?" Luisa asked.

"Pooped," Emma said.

"Did you see the truck?" Luisa asked.

"What truck?" Emma said.

Luisa pointed. "That one!"

Emma sat up and looked around. In the parking lot behind them was a big white truck with a thing on the top like a satellite dish. On the side of the truck were the letters *WMJN*. And next to the truck stood a couple of people, including a man with a camera.

"Is that a TV crew?" Emma asked.

Luisa nodded. "I heard Mr. George tell one of the moms that he thinks the Rockets told them to come. The Rockets are show-offs, you know."

"Ha!" Emma said. "They don't have anything to show off about. We've stopped them so far."

"*You* stopped them," Luisa said. "You're awesome

at goal."

"I'm better at scoring," Emma said.

Luisa didn't answer.

"Aren't I?" Emma asked.

Luisa looked away. "You're good at both," she said.

"Thanks," said Emma. But she wondered if Luisa really meant that. And then Emma thought of something. She turned back and studied the TV crew. Was that Mrs. Beene standing there with them? It seemed to be. *Cool!* she thought. They had come to take pictures of *her*! To do a story about *her*. And then she realized that's why Katie was stretching like that, posing for the cameras.

"Luisa!" she said, grabbing Luisa's shirt and tugging on it. "That's Mrs. Beene. The one I told you about from yesterday, remember? You think the camera crew is here to take pictures of me for her story?"

Luisa turned and looked. "Wow!" she said. "That would be *excellent*."

Emma nodded. "It would be," she said. And then she added, "I don't think it could be, though. I mean, I don't think so."

"I do," Luisa said, and she grinned at Emma. "So now we *have* to win!"

Emma smiled back. She could feel her heart

thudding really hard. A story about her! Maybe she'd even be on TV. She reached behind her and grabbed a towel to dry her soaking wet hair. And that's when she noticed something—not the TV people. She noticed that Annie was frantically waving to her. Annie was mouthing something, too.

Marmaduke! It looked as if she were saying Marmaduke!

Ohmygosh! Had he gotten out of his cage? Or . . .

And then she remembered. Marmaduke! They had all forgotten Marmaduke.

Emma scrambled off the ground. "Luisa!" she said, grabbing Luisa's hand and pulling her up. She reached for Margaret Ann, too. "Come on!" she said. "Marmaduke! We forgot about Marmaduke."

"What about him?" Luisa asked.

"We forgot to pat him! For good luck!"

"Ohmygosh," Luisa said. "We did."

And they had. With all the fussing and worrying about Margaret Ann's badge, nobody had remembered to pet Marmaduke's nose!

"Everybody!" Emma yelled. She jumped around, waving her arms madly. "Everybody. Come here! Marmaduke! We forgot to pet Marmaduke."

The girls leaped to their feet. They dropped their

towels and water bottles and oranges. And, as if they were all one person, the whole pack of them went racing along the sidelines. Even Katie ran along.

Rats! Emma thought.

"Marmaduke's been looking for you!" Annie said when they got there, all out of breath. "He's been waiting."

"How could we forget!" Emma said. She dropped to her knees by Marmaduke's cage. "Marmaduke!" she murmured. "How could we have forgotten you?"

All of the girls huddled around. They murmured and fussed over him. One by one, they reached into his cage to pet his nose. He snuffled and made little snorty noises at them. Every single player stuck a finger into the cage.

"Girls!" Mr. George called. "Get over here. Almost time."

"Coming!" Emma yelled.

The girls got back on their feet. Emma stayed kneeling for just one more minute.

"Marmaduke," she said softly. She puckered up her lips and stuck her face up against the cage bars. She gave him a kiss on the nose. "We need you, buddy!" she whispered.

He snuffled and kissed her back.

And then she and all the others ran back to the game. When she got to the field, she looked over her shoulder for a second. She saw that Annie had taken Marmaduke out of his cage. She was holding him up to her shoulder so he could see the game, too.

Now they'd be sure to have good luck!

Chapter Fourteen
Marmaduke to the Rescue

Except maybe they wouldn't. Because they couldn't score. No matter what they did, no matter how hard they played, they could not score a goal.

The only good thing was that the Rockets couldn't score, either. Both teams raced up and down the field, up and down, as if they were wired.

Emma kept looking around to see where the TV crew was. Were they watching the whole team? Or just her? And how was she supposed to stand out? And what if the only person who scored was Katie? Would they write the whole story about Katie instead?

Midway into the second half, the coach for the Rockets was acting like a lunatic. He was practically screaming at his team. He kept jumping up and down and yelling, "Keep your head in the game! Keep your head in the game."

At one point, he took off his hat and threw it on the ground. Emma bent over, her hands on her knees, catching her breath. "Help us, Marmaduke," she whispered. "Help us."

Suddenly, Emma saw that Katie had an opening down the field. She had the ball all to herself. She was running like the wind, weaving in and out of defenders. There was just one defender left in front of her. She wasn't off-side. She had the ball, juggling it foot to foot.

Great footwork, Emma thought, and then hated that she was thinking that.

But she couldn't help it. Katie was awesome. She seemed as if she were on an Olympic team, darting, weaving. The defender was backing up in front of her, trying to snag the ball from her.

But Katie was too swift. She ran. She turned. She paused. The defender paused.

Katie made a quick dart to the right. Then to the left.

The defender danced around in front of her.

Katie dribbled more. Left. Right. Hard move right. And then, while the defender was still going right, Katie kicked left. A hard, hard kick. The goalie was poised, both hands out, in the dead center of the goal . . . while Katie drove the ball toward the far left corner.

But the Rockets' goalie was just too quick. She made a dive to the left, leaping into the air as if she had wings. She tipped the ball up, up. It came down. Touched her hand. She tipped it again. It flipped up. And then bounced down—down into her hands. She had it. She tumbled to the ground on top of it.

Emma screamed with frustration. And then she was happy. But then she felt bad for being happy. She thought of what Mr. George had said when she and Katie had been arguing before. "This is a team! Or, at least, it's supposed to be."

So she shouted, "Good try!" at Katie.

The pace of the game picked up again. And then something wonderful happened: Luisa scored. She had a nice, clear, open field to the goal, and she kicked from way over near the sidelines. The ball slammed past the goalie and snapped hard into the net.

Everyone jumped up and down and cheered. Then the ref stepped in with his flag. Off-side! No goal.

Luisa looked downfield at Emma. Her shoulders sagged. She shrugged. Emma gave her a thumbs-up. "It's okay!" she shouted. "Try again!"

But the whole second half went like that. Katie almost had another goal but, once again, the goalie fell on it and trapped it.

Finally, twenty minutes—or a thousand minutes—later, the whistle blew. Time was up. The game was over. And it was still tied at zero to zero.

There would be a five-minute break. And then sudden-death overtime.

Emma and the rest of the team collapsed on the sidelines.

The way it was going to work was this: All the girls on the Hornets would line up. One person would be chosen to kick the ball toward the goal. There would be no defenders—just the Rockets' goalie all by herself. She had to stop the kick. If the Hornets scored—or even if they didn't—the ball went to the other end of the field. Then the Rockets got a chance to kick.

They would keep on doing that, giving each team a chance in each round, until one team got a goal and the other team didn't. The team that got the goal won.

"Okay, Hornets," Mr. George said, gathering the girls in a circle around him. "You've done a great job. Just a few minutes to go. We can do this. Right?"

They all nodded.

Emma was breathing hard, and her heart was

hammering away like crazy. She looked around the circle. Who was Mr. George going to choose to kick the goal for them? She knew it couldn't be her. So she hoped, she hoped, she hoped like anything it would be Luisa.

Luisa was looking at Mr. George.

Katie was looking at Mr. George.

Everybody was looking at Mr. George.

Mr. George was looking down at his clipboard.

After what seemed like forever, he glanced up. His eyes went around the circle. He tossed the clipboard to the ground behind him. He clapped his hands.

"Let's go, girls. Take the field," he said. And then he said, "Katie! You're up."

Somebody groaned. A couple of people made sounds as if they were surprised. But they all trotted out to the field, side by side.

Emma moved beside Luisa. "I'm sorry," she said.

Luisa nodded. She didn't look at Emma. Emma thought maybe she was going to cry. "It's okay," Emma whispered. "Honest. You are the best."

Luisa nodded again.

The Hornets lined up, shoulder to shoulder, facing the Rockets' goal. Katie stood in the center of the line. The defender for the Rockets crouched in the goal. She had fierce-looking eyes, eyes that darted like piranhas, this way and that.

Katie took her stance. She held the ball between her feet. She shifted back and forth, back and forth.

Emma made her hands into little fists. She held her breath. She didn't know what she wished for. She hated that Katie would be the hero. But she also wanted so much for the Hornets to win. She thought of DC and the trophy. She watched as slowly, Katie moved forward, slowly, slowly.

Suddenly, Katie wasn't moving slowly anymore. She charged forward, then made a terrific sliding side kick. The ball flew crosswise across the net. The defender threw herself at it. She touched it, just like last time. It bobbled off the tips of her fingers. Just like last time. It leaped. She leaped. It kept spinning. But this time, she didn't catch it. It spun away. And dribbled into the far corner of the net. Goal!

The Hornets cheered. Emma pumped her arms in the air. They were ahead.

Except now she was up.

The Rockets moved to the far end of the field. Emma ran to her place at the goal. She couldn't even run; she was so exhausted. She just sort of trotted like a very tired horse.

Emma took her place in the goal. She didn't know if she could do this. She was so tired, her legs felt like rubber, hot rubber.

The Rockets lined up facing her. Emma could feel her heart thundering away. She swallowed hard and wished she'd drunk some more of that water she'd poured on her head.

Roberta, the biggest Rocket girl, took the ball. The age limit for this league was nine years and younger, but Roberta looked twenty. She was tall, with long red hair tied back in a fat ponytail.

Emma was afraid. But only a little bit. She knew how to handle Roberta. She thought she did. She had already stopped three kicks from her during the game. She knew Roberta's trick. *Watch her eyes,* she said to herself, *not the ball. Watch where Roberta is looking. And then you'll know where she is going to kick.*

Emma concentrated hard. Hard. Roberta's eyes went left. Then right. Then left again. She dribbled left. Then right. Then left again. Definitely left.

Emma felt she was being tricked. So she watched the right side.

And bam! The ball flew at her—directly at her— to her right. Exactly where she had expected it. She leaped and stopped it—in mid-air.

The Hornets screamed. The parents cheered. Emma thought even some of the Rockets' parents might have cheered. She wasn't sure. But she had done it. She had won the game.

Well, maybe not.

Maybe Katie had won the game.

All the girls gathered around her, hugging and screaming. Mr. George grabbed her, hugged her, and then threw her up in the air. Then he hugged Katie. Everybody was acting nuts. Even the camera people were crowding out onto the field.

Emma was grinning and grinning. And then she had a funny, sad little feeling. She wished Ira hadn't been sick. She wished Mom had been there to see.

Still, she had won. They'd been together—a team. And Katie was looking at her. Katie, who had scored the winning goal.

Emma took a deep breath.

Katie was walking over to her.

"You did good," Katie said, stopping in front of her. She twirled her hair around her index finger and seemed kind of shy. "Really. I mean, you're good at goalie. And striker, too."

Emma nodded. She swallowed. "Thanks," she said. "You were good, too. You won the game."

"I know," Katie said. "I mean, I didn't. I mean . . . we both did. Didn't we?" And then she smiled at Emma, and it seemed like a real smile, not a mean one.

Emma smiled back. She was thinking about what Mr. George had said—about their being a team. And they *were* a team. They had played like a team.

Emma turned and walked over to the sidelines. But as she walked, she couldn't help thinking: I just wish I could like Katie a little bit more.

Chapter Fifteen
All Is Well

O'Fallon Kids Are On Strike

That was the headline on the front page of the paper the following morning. And it was followed by the story:

When the five O'Fallon kids, led by nine-year-old Emma, realized that events in their household were not to their liking, they decided to take matters into their own hands. They did something that few ordinary children might do: they went on strike.

But Emma O'Fallon is no ordinary girl. A bright, gutsy little dynamo, Emma led her brothers and sisters on a picket line on a foggy, rainy afternoon last Sunday, determined to make their parents, Mr. and Mrs. O'Fallon, address some of their concerns. They created signs listing their demands. Three of their demands revolved around their wish to be allowed to keep a new kitten and a new ferret, temporarily in the care of their nanny, Annie O'Reilly. Emma O'Fallon also addressed the issue of who would be a chaperone for the Hornets, the local traveling soccer team. . . .

Emma smiled. She had already read the story about a zillion times. The whole family had read it, except for the little ones who couldn't read. Emma had read it out loud to them. There were pictures with the article, too, pictures of all five kids and a picture of Kelley.

On the inside page was another whole story about Emma and her team and soccer. It told a whole lot about Marmaduke, the team's good-luck charm.

Without Marmaduke, would the Hornets really have won? Was it just a coincidence that only after all the girls had petted him, they finally got a score?

The stories weren't just about Emma and Marmaduke, though. Nor were they just about her being the star player—the best. They were about the whole team. And the whole family. For some reason, Emma didn't mind that. At least, not too much. She had begun to think that a team and a family were a lot alike.

Mrs. Beene had written that she wondered how the family would settle the strike. And now Daddy, back from his short trip, had set up a time for everyone to do just that—talk.

Negotiate, Emma said inside her head.

The whole family and Annie were settled around the table, the kitchen table, because it was round. Daddy had chosen that because, he said, smiling at Emma, that way it wouldn't seem as if anyone was in charge. If you had a regular table and one person was at the head of it, it would seem as if that person were the boss. Emma sometimes thought that Daddy was very smart.

Emma sat between Annie and Tim. Mom sat next to Daddy. The little kids were there, too, wiggling around in their seats and jabbering to one another. Ira and Lizzie had completely forgotten their fight from the other day.

"Okay," Daddy said, "what's first on the agenda?"

"Kelley!" McClain said.

"Marshmallow!" Ira and Lizzie said together.

"Let's do one thing at a time," Emma said. "Kelley first."

"Okay," Daddy said. "What about her?"

"Well," Emma said. "I just think that Kelley— well, I mean, I can understand that you and Mom might not want a cat, but . . ."

"That's not nice!" McClain said.

"Hush, McClain," Emma said. "But why can't McClain go upstairs and visit Kelley? I mean, if Annie says it's okay with her, why isn't it okay with you?"

"It's just that it was so wild last weekend," Mom said slowly. "I mean, with Annie getting home and you kids out in your pajamas in the middle of the night and Woof barking and then having another ferret run loose in the house when we already have one that keeps escaping. And then, a strange kitten! For heaven's sake, like we need a cat! And . . ."

"I know," Tim said quietly. "It is kind of a crazy house."

"And I was worried about the strike," Daddy said.

"So maybe we overreacted," Mom said.

"But can we, I mean, can Annie keep Kelley and

Marshmallow? And can we visit them?" asked Emma.

Mom turned to Annie. "It's up to you, Annie," she said.

"Oh, I'd love to have the darling pets," Annie said. "And I love to have the children visit me and them upstairs. If that's all right with you, I mean."

"But can they come down at all?" Emma asked. "Marshmallow and Kelley, I mean? And be downstairs at least a little bit? They won't be wild, honest. And I won't let Marshmallow get out of her cage."

"And I won't let Kelley and Woof fight," McClain said. She had her hands folded as if she were praying. Even Ira and Lizzie were holding very still, staring intently at Mom and Daddy.

"Please, please, please," McClain whispered.

Daddy looked at Mom. Mom looked back. They both sighed. They shook their heads. And then, they both burst out laughing.

"Why not!" Mom said. She waved her hand. "Like Tim just said, it's already a crazy household."

"All right!" McClain said.

"Yippee!" Lizzie said.

"Awesome!" Ira said.

Emma laughed. She had never heard Ira say that before. But then she sat up very straight. She took a deep breath. Now the important stuff was coming.

"Okay," she said. "Mom and Daddy, you said it would be good for Annie to visit DC 'cause she'd never been there before."

Mom and Daddy looked at one another. Daddy nodded. Mom did, too. But Mom did it more slowly. She looked a little sad. Or maybe worried. Something.

"And Marmaduke?" Mom said. She tapped the newspaper with her finger. "I presume you want to take Marmaduke?"

Emma looked away. She bit her lip. Marmaduke had to go. She was so afraid that Mom would say no. But maybe, now that Mrs. Beene had written about the traveling team and added the bit about how much Marmaduke was needed for good luck, Mom would say yes. Still . . .

She looked up. Mom was smiling.

"I can?" Emma said.

Mom nodded. "I'm probably insane, but . . ." She shrugged and turned to Daddy. "Is there any chance in the whole world that Marmaduke won't escape while he's in DC?"

Probably not, Emma thought.

Daddy shrugged. But then he said, "Does the hotel allow pets?"

"I already checked," Mom said. "They do."

Inside, Emma felt totally surprised. Mom had given in so easily. And she had even called to check with the hotel. Was it because of the story in the paper? Or . . . ?

"I'll take care of Marshmallow and Kelley," Tim said. "While Emma's gone."

"Kelley's mine," McClain said. "But I'll let you help."

"We'll help with Marshmallow," Lizzie said. "Right, Ira?"

Mom turned to Annie. "Annie," she said, "you'll take good care of them all, won't you? All the girls?"

"Of course," Annie answered.

"I don't mean just the medical business," Mom said. "I know you can manage that. I mean, you'll all have fun? It's not just about winning games, you know."

Annie nodded. "It's about lots more than that," she said. She turned to Emma. "Right, Emma?"

Emma nodded. Mom was right. Annie was right. It was about more than just winning games. And being the best. It was about . . . what? Being a team?

She didn't know. But something was niggling around in her head, and it had to do with Mom. For some reason, Emma suddenly remembered her feeling on the field the other day—how she had wished Mom had been there to see the great save she had made.

And then she thought of something else. Why hadn't she thought of it before? She had wondered why Mom had wanted so much to go to DC with her. She had thought it was because Mom didn't trust her and wanted to keep an eye on her. But maybe it wasn't that at all. Maybe Mom just wanted to be with her. To be part of the whole thing. And she had been pushing Mom away and begging for Annie and . . .

"So you guys have fun together," Mom went on. She turned to Emma. "And tell me all about it when you get home."

Emma slid down from her chair. She went around the table and stood beside Mom. She looked at Annie.

Annie grinned.

"Mom?" Emma said. "It's only for two days. And it's a weekend, and Daddy could take care of the little kids. Tim would help. So could you come with Annie and me?"

Mom frowned. "What do you mean?"

"Come with me. With both Annie and me," Emma said. "Why not? You'd have fun."

"But—Annie's going," Mom said.

"So?" Emma said.

Mom began smiling. And then she looked a little weird. It seemed almost as if . . . no, she wasn't crying. She couldn't be crying. She was laughing. She actually was laughing. She looked across the table at Daddy.

"Could you manage?" she asked.

Daddy turned to Tim and raised his eyebrows a little. "If I get some help."

Tim nodded. "Definitely." He smiled and ducked his head. "If I get my cell phone."

Daddy laughed. "We'll see," he said. He turned to the little kids. They all looked up at him.

"Sure!" Daddy said. "Piece of cake."

"I love cake!" Ira said.

"Then I'd love to go," Mom said, looking at Emma. "I'd really love to."

"Yippee!" Emma said, and she gave Mom a hug, a big, fat hug.

Then she looked around the room—at Tim and McClain and Ira and Lizzie, at Mom and Daddy and Annie. She felt something big swell up inside her, something important, something—happy. And though she couldn't say just what it was, she knew it was good. She wasn't the star. She didn't need to be. They were all stars. They were a family. A team.

And she didn't need a trophy to prove it.